## Summary

This book, The Mourning Dove Takes Flight, is the final installment in the Mourning Dove Trilogy. The first book, Call of the Mourning Dove, introduces us to Reverend Simon Morris and his life in Southern Rhodesia in the mid 1900's. It describes his trials and triumphs during the colonial era. The story picks up in the early 1980's with The Mourning Dove Calls Again, where we meet Maggie who has just returned to what is now called Zimbabwe. The dramatic shift in the political scene there disrupts and destroys many lives.

Now, in The Mourning Doves Takes Flight, we meet young Sammy who is forced to leave all he has ever known. With his aunt Maggie, he moves to a different country and has to learn to embrace the changes. The tension between Maggie and her old college friend, Peter Nell, starts to deteriorate after Sammy has to spend time under his care. Sammy has the support of his African friend Rosie who, like many others, has moved to South Africa with the hopes of a better life.

Maggie and her love, Bento, decide to make a clean break from the ties of Africa. With Sammy, they move to the United States. Being immersed in a different way of life on a different continent brings both rewards and hardships. Bento's father, Jeffrey as well as the long time friends Sugar, Chaz, and their son Morris are the support this new family needs.

As the years pass, both Morris and Sammy are drawn back to the land of their births, in the hope of healing the wounds of the past and closing unresolved relationships. Their love of Africa is deeply rooted, even though they have been raised in different cultures. Can they embrace forgiveness and create lives of honor and purpose? When they return to the place of their births, the mourning dove in the giant marula tree repeats the question that was asked of their ancestors: Croo-croo-croo: What will you choose, what will you choose?

*Illustrations by Fran Webster*

# The Mourning Dove

# Takes Flight

## A Novel

Christine M. Gordon

Cover Art by Fran Webster

# DEDICATION

To family and friends, scattered far and wide.

To the essence of Africa indelibly etched into my soul.

# ACKNOWLEDGMENTS

Many thanks, to those that kept encouraging me to write this story.

Special thanks to Ruth Gordon who was instrumental in having it completed, with her editing, formatting, and constant support.

Thank you to my sister Lorraine Albasini and my niece Tareen Albasini-Boyce for keeping the story on track.

Thank you to Fran Webster who gave beauty to the pages with her amazing sketches that are instilled with the love of Africa.

Thank you to my daughter, Shayla Gordon, for her encouragement.

Thank you to Melodie Johnson-Howe and Marilyn Brissette for their editorial contributions.

# TABLE OF CONTENTS

## Introduction

A young boy flies away from his homeland, Zimbabwe. Memories of family and his place of birth sustain him as he, like many others leaves the country to forge a new life. Africa is still his home for many years. As the political scene in South Africa begins to shift, he is thrust into more change, this time on a different continent and in a different culture. He learns to embrace the changes and recreates a life balancing his new world with the values from his place of birth.

## 1. The Flight

I remembered the feel of the cool, hard glass against my skin as my cheek pressed to the surface of the small, oval window.  Sounds I had never heard before whooshed around and around my aching ears--the air conditioner in the vent high above me; the sound of the throb, throb of engines of the huge South African Airways airplane--pulsed through my body taking me away, far away from all that I had known in my six years.

I had struggled with the seatbelt tightly holding me in place and the stuffed toy, my beloved brown moose, squished against my belly. I readjusted him gently.

"How are you doing Sammy?" Aunt Maggie asked as she reached over from her seat next to me to take my hand, and then patted my head.  Her fingers paused and lightly touched the cowlick at my forehead.

She sighed as her hands brushed through her strawberry blond hair.  "We will be taking off very soon and they will be bringing us some food and then you can take a nap and guess what?  We will be in Durban before you know it, and I bet we will be able to see the ocean before we land."

Squinting against the glare of the blinding sun reflecting sharp shards of light zinging against the metal wing, I could just see the figure standing on the airport balcony, one arm raised high in a goodbye wave.  It was not my father.  My mother was not there.  Away, away.  Far away.  They had gone.

"Mama.  I want my mama," I had cried quietly to myself, as the airplane hurdled forward faster and faster, screaming louder and louder.

I had cupped my hands over my ears and swallowed and gulped, trying to ease the squeezing pain in my ears.  I remembered the way my stomach jumped and wriggled like a chongololo, then, as if touched lightly by a tiny finger, curled tightly into a protective hard ball.  The golden landscape started to fall away as we rose into the huge, open sky.  Gripping the armrest with all my might, I tried to hold in a sob that cried out for things to go back in time.  As we lifted higher, I saw the mottled shadows of msasa trees against the bushland grow smaller and fade into a blur.  All I wanted was to go back to my home--to go back to the farm.

To remember… playing in the red, Zimbabwe soil with trucks and Dinky cars, the warm sun melting away any thoughts but following those imaginary looping roads through rocky outcrops on the Nata Reserve.  To remember… the bitter smell of wood fire filtering from the cast iron stove in the kitchen and layered upon that, the rich, yeasty aroma of bread pulled hot from the oven.

I remembered sounds the most; chickens squawking their disapproval as Mama, her long, fair hair fluttering in the humid breeze, took the warm, brown eggs from the coop and cradled them carefully in her floral apron.

"One for Papa, one for Mama and one for Sammy too," she would always sing.  "Don't forget to thank the hukus, Sam my boy," she would add with a laugh.

There was the low call of doves high in the acacia tree, the moo-mooing, and the piercing whistles of the herd boys as they brought the cattle back to the pens with the rosy glow of sundown broadening shadows into beautiful, weird shapes.  Whack, whack, whack.  Sharp axe met hard wood.  The laughter and singing of African voices rising from the compound; the notes of the tribal songs stacked one upon another; deep male voices and lilting melodies offered by the women--the rhythm seemed to pulse within me like blood pumping through my veins.

I remembered those sounds.  Sounds etched into my soul.  Those wisps of my past, flowing faintly back, as if from another life.

## 2. A New Life
### Durban, South Africa  1986

Aunt Maggie and I lived upstairs in a small, two-bedroom flat.  It was several blocks away from Durban Beach.

"Sammy, how do you like this bedspread?" Maggie unfolded the blue and red checked cover for my twin bed.  "I found it at Pep store.  I think it will brighten the place up, don't you?"

"Sure.  It will be okay," I answered.  "Do you think we can get a place to put my clothes?  That cupboard is really small."

We had each brought a couple of suitcases on the flight from Zimbabwe.  Most of my things had been left at the farm.  The only special thing that I had been able to bring on the plane was my stuffed moose; the one Maggie had sent from Canada when I was a baby.  Maggie had brought nothing except her clothes.

"Maggie, won't you miss the things that you had in Canada?  Can you go back and get them?"

My aunt chuckled, but her eyes seemed sad.  She sat on the bed and looked around the room.  There wasn't much else in it.  We had put a few pictures on the wall and bought a wooden chair and a rug.  She pushed back her hair.  I loved the colour of it, even though it was so different from Mama.  It was a rosy, goldy colour and had this kind of wave to it.

"It's a very long way back to Canada, Sammy.  It would cost more money to fly there than to buy the things we need here.  There is nothing that I will miss that much.  My friend Sugar will be there for a while and she will pack up a few important things for me.  She can just hold onto them.  I'm sure I'll see her and Chaz after they get married.  I know they will come back to Africa someday."

"Why did you want to come to South Africa and not go back to Canada?" I asked, plopping myself down on the bed next to her.

She turned to look at me and her hand reached up and stroked my hair.  She let out a heavy sigh.

"Sammy, I promised your Mom I would take care of you."  She swallowed.  "It's kind of complicated, but the Canadian Government wouldn't let me bring you back to live there, and we couldn't stay in Zimbabwe, after all that happened."  She paused.  "My friend Peter, well, he can help us out a bit, so South Africa it is!"  She chuckled dryly.

We both sat quietly for a while, lost in our thoughts.  We had fumbled into a relationship, this aunt of mine who I had never met before she had come to take care of me.  Her voice so like my mother's at times that I would call out to her, "Mama, Mama!"  But then I'd notice that her hair was not the shiny colour of the savannah grass; it was not Mama's tinkling laugh.  Mama was gone.  Papa was gone; both killed in a brutal raid on the farm in Zimbabwe and that life was no more.

There were trees and gardens and the sea was within walking distance, but it was not the open, vast spaces that I had loved so much.  The sounds were different here--cars and buses, the buzz of lawnmowers and screeching police car sirens.

I longed for the soothing croo-croo of the doves that used to serenade me as I woke up to the sun rising brightly in a big, big sky.  I missed the low, almost plaintive bleating of the goats as the herd boys whistled them home to the kraal; the sun slipping below the curve of the warm, sun-baked earth.

I had never been to school, having taken my lessons outside under the trees with Mama and two of the older herd boys.  We would count the leaves and stones; the soldier ants as they marched in long black columns.  We would write with sticks in the dusty, red soil and joyfully clap out rhythms and sing songs to learn our ABC's, in the boys' native language, Sindebele, and English.

Now, it seemed that I wasn't allowed to even speak with the "blacks," as people called them. I had to squeeze into a scratchy school uniform and sit still at a hard, wooden desk and learn numbers and words that I already knew. I was always getting a rap on my knuckles to wake me up from my daydreaming.

Maggie's voice interrupted my thoughts. "Sammy, you know I have to change my hours at work now, so I've asked Peter to help us out."

She stood up from the bed, walked over to the wooden chair and started folding the pile of laundry stacked on it.

"You can ride over to his house after school until I can pick you up. It will be around five o'clock. That will be okay, won't it?"

"I guess. When is Bento coming back? Can't he look after me?"

Bento and I had spent countless hours playing on the Durban beach, and going to the library where he introduced me to art. Now, the memory of Bento waving goodbye to us at the Harare Airport was sadly etched in my mind.

Maggie smiled and her face grew soft. I knew she liked her boyfriend a lot!

"Bento will be in Portugal for quite a long time. He has to finish teaching his art classes at the university there. Then he will be able to retire and come to join us in South Africa. Did I show you the picture he just sent me?" She slipped her hand into her skirt pocket and pulled out an envelope.

I walked over to her and she handed me a photograph. Bento was tossing something into a fountain and his thick, dark hair was being blown about in the wind.

"He said he was making a wish that he would soon be with us," Maggie said laughing.

I smiled. "I like Bento a lot. He is really cool. It will be great when he is here."

"Hmmm. I do too," Maggie said.

"Did you meet Bento in Canada?"

"Oh no," Maggie said with a smile. "I only met him in Zimbabwe. I was visiting Victoria Falls." She laughed again. "I walked into him. Slam!" She clapped her hands together. "…and fell to the floor. I think I must have fainted for a minute and he was so worried!"

She paused and looked across at me, the unfolded sheet draping from her arms.

"You know Sammy, the only thing that makes the loss of your Mama at all bearable is that now I have you and Bento in my life."

She was silent for a long time.

"Come on then, my boy and help me with this never-ending laundry."  She tossed one of my t-shirts over to me and gave a thumbs-up when I caught it.

## 3. My Friend Rosie

It wasn't that Maggie's friend Peter had ever hurt me but I wondered what he would he be like.  I didn't know what was worse, school and teachers that didn't seem to understand me, or arriving at Peter's.

At one o'clock I would escape from the forlorn, brick walls of the school.  With the wind ruffling my hair, I would speed away on my rickety bicycle to spend the afternoon with him while Aunt Maggie finished work.

I propped my bike against the tall bougainvillea hedge, where a cascade of low-hanging runners filled with fiery red flowers, grasped for my hair and the sharp thorns pulled at my school uniform.  I wriggled free and slowly struggled with the heavy, spiked wrought iron gates.  With a clank they slammed shut; keeping, we hoped, the threats of theft and harm away.

A slate path led up to the front door, winding its way through a garden set with beds of bright daisies and tall lilies.  I could hear the soft sound of bees making their dutiful way to each blossom.  Perched in the jacaranda tree, in the centre of the somewhat green lawn, the hadeda birds, hidden by the purple clusters of flowers, were making their raucous noise: har, har, har.  The house, with its red bricks covered in green creepers, was low and sprawling, nestling comfortably into its one-acre plot. I stepped up to the door and on the tips of my toes stretched for the brass ring that came down thump, thump against the wooden door. I swallowed and waited. There was no sound. I counted in my head slowly, one, two, three, four, five. I strained again to lift the doorknocker and down it came again. Thump. Then there was a shuffling and slapping of bare feet on tile. I heard the lock click, and the door creaked open.

"Ah, Sammy. Come now. Shoosh, shoosh. Baas Peter he resting now," Rosie said as she opened the door.

Her round, shiny black face was creased into a frown. Her checked pink dress strained over her large frame and under the pink doek on her head, a few tight black curls peeked out. She ushered me into the hallway, and we crept towards the living room.

The room was dim, as the curtains had been pulled over the sliding glass door that led onto the veranda. I could just make out the propped up body of Peter sprawled in the blue velvet armchair. His eyes were closed and soft snoring slipped from his open mouth. I paused at the door, waiting for Rosie who had, despite her ample bulk, glided in and made her way towards the inert form. She reached down and collected several brown glass bottles that were close to the chair. The loud clinks had me hold my breath and I quickly glanced at Rosie. Our eyes met. Peter grunted and flicked his hand towards his face, as if brushing away some pesky fly then sighed and continued his slumber. Rosie put a finger over her mouth, urging me to stay still and quiet. She gave a slight smile and in a pantomime of stealth, tiptoed out of the room. We hurried to the kitchen.

"Maiwee," she laughed. "Is too much shumba for that one, yes sir!"

"What do you mean, Rosie?" I asked. "I know shumba is a lion. Why is a lion too much for Uncle Peter?"

She rattled the bottles together and then I noticed the picture on the label and the words LION LAGER.

"Iziko induba, Sam-Sam." She gave me a soft, sad smile while patting my head.

She put a glass of milk and a white bread, Fray Bentos sandwich on the red Formica kitchen table. She placed a cushion on the matching chair and helped me sit just tall enough to reach my snack. She retrieved the Dick and Jane reader from the small, polka-dotted suitcase I took to school.

"Come and eat now and read your book."

The ironing board, iron, and large basket of laundry were pulled from the scullery.  We settled to our tasks, waiting for the yell from the living room, "ROOOOOSIEEEE," that would indicate that the Lion Lager had been slept off and the baas was awake.

## 4. Lady in the Moon

My eyes were smarting in the dim, smoke-filled room. I covered them with my hands, attempting to shut out the irritating Johnny Walker sign that flashed its neon message on-and-off and on-and-off. A headache started to settle heavily at the top of my skull. The sound of the Bee Gees plaintively asking, "How deep is your love?" could just be heard above the noise of tink-tinkling bottles, coarse laughter, and gruff male voices. I stifled a yawn and curled up tighter in the old, lumpy armchair that was tucked into a corner of the country club bar.

My friend Evan perched in the chair across from me. "It's your turn to go and ask. I got the peanuts out of my dad. Go on, ask Peter for something. I'm starving," he pleaded.

His eyes glinted from behind his wire-rimmed glasses and he brushed his auburn hair away from his face. The skinny kid with large ears and a whiney voice was the only friend I had made at school. We had started hanging out together after finding ourselves stuck in the corner of the bar on numerous evenings; waiting....

"Jeez, I really don't want to ask him now," I complained as my belly rumbled with hunger.

I gazed hopefully, to see if the glass in front of Peter was getting closer to empty. His back was to me as he slumped onto the counter, half-sitting on the heavy wooden bar stool. He was conversing in deep concentration with the rugged-looking man beside him. The bar was crowded. Businessmen still in suits, mixed in with the polo shirt crowd fresh from the golf course, either celebrating their success or washing away their disappointment in the battle with a small, white, dimpled ball. Sweaty, grass-streaked, mud-splattered rugby players stood slurping their Castle Lagers and thumping each other on the back for a game well played.

I could see Peter's face in the reflection of the large, somewhat clouded mirror behind the bar. My heart sank. His eyes were drooping and that tell-tale blush on his cheeks and constant 'swatting away flies,' as I called it, indicating that this was going to be one of those nights.

"Okay. I'm going!"

I knew that if I waited and I interrupted Peter any later, I would be sent packing and told to "stop bloody interrupting me boy..." with perhaps a swat on the arm or a push away, depending on the number of drinks consumed.

I had never tested the limit to see if he would actually hit me. I must have known to keep my mouth shut and stay out of range. Because it was Saturday night, this would be a late one. I had to do it now. I crept forward through the throng of bodies towards the bar counter.

"Hey Peter, excuse me." I stepped in between him and the scary-looking man. "I hope you don't mind, but can I get something to eat?"

Peter turned towards me and paused for a moment. His eyes were glazed and he shook his head as if trying to figure out who, or what I was. He hiccupped and then patted me on the head.

"Sammy, my boy, you still here, huh? You hungry?"

I held my breath and nodded, not trusting my voice. Less said the better.

"Phineas, my friend, you got a Cornish pasty for Sammy?"

I could just make out the bartender's face hovering above the counter. He looked tired and his dark face glowed with sweat. He looked down at me with a sad smile.

"Sorry, Baas, kitchen is closed now. I just have potato chips and biltong."

"Alright, give the boy what he wants. Don't overcharge me now, you skelm!" Peter turned away from me and I walked to the end of the counter.

Phineas gave me a wink and handed me two packets of chips, a long stick of biltong and two bottles of Coke. "Next time you come and find me quick–quick, okay Sam? You and Evan too skinny with no dinners. I just get it for you. Baas he forget."

I grabbed my loot and headed back to Evan who grinned as he saw me coming.

"Wow, you scored tonight," he said cheerfully.

I placed the meal on the coffee table and sighed. That had been easy. This time. Got to time it right, I thought to myself as I tore open the packet and savoured the tart salt and vinegar chips.

Evan and I, our stomachs a little fuller, had started another round of Snap when a large shadow swayed above us. His father gazed down and without a word, grabbed Evan by the ear and hauled him to his feet. Evan followed his dad's stumbling gait reluctantly. He turned and gave me a quick wave before they disappeared into the dark night.

I felt sad for Evan. He was headed home to more trouble. His mother was a mean old tannie who would give the old man hell and probably clip Evan around the ears as if he had anything to do with the lateness of the hour and condition of his dad.

At least I had Aunt Maggie and Bento. They had been together since we had left Zimbabwe. I remembered seeing him wave goodbye at the Harare Airport as we flew away four long years ago. He had finally moved to South Africa. Over the years, he had been back to Portugal a couple of times. He had just returned and had taken Maggie to Cape Town for a holiday. As I thought about having to stay with Peter for the week, my stomach ached and I felt a smarting in my eyes, far more intense than that smoke-filled hellhole could provide.

"Bloody hell, Maggie. Thanks a lot for taking off on my birthday." I revelled in the cuss words. No one in the bar could hear me, so I repeated them. "Bloody hell!"

Would Aunt Maggie have washed my mouth out with soap if she had heard? I doubted it. Not like Evan's mom who had half-drowned him at the sink and scrubbed his mouth out with Sunlight soap.

The birthday celebration Peter had planned filled me with dread. Ten years old.

"What do you want for your birthday?" Peter had asked.

How about leaving sucky South Africa and going home to Zimbabwe?  How about seeing those friends I had spent so much time with on the farm, the ones I could count on no matter what colour their skin was?  How about having a mom and dad to share it with?

I must have drifted off to sleep.  The music woke me.  Someone had turned up the volume and some old country song was playing. The noise level in the bar was louder too.  A few women's voices were layered over the din and as I peered out of sleepy eyes, the scene looked like something from an old western saloon.  A couple was attempting to dance in the crowded space, the drinks in their hands slopping on the floor as they twirled.  Bottles of beer were being passed over the heads of those close to the bar to the press of bodies behind them.

I slipped from my seat and half-asleep, scurried towards the door. I didn't look back to see where Peter was.  I pushed my way out with a sigh of relief.  It felt good as I took in a big breath of sweet air.  I gasped as I looked up into that night sky.  A feeling I couldn't describe washed over me--sadness, disappointment, and emptiness. There was a brilliant full moon peeking from behind a cloud.  A couple of trees bathed in the light.  I stood for a moment in awe.  She was so bright and glowy.  Light seemed to shine from her; soft rays that flowed like Mama's beautiful hair.  I wanted to stretch my arms up and up, to reach out to touch her.  The silky softness; the ripple of soft satin under my fingers, remembering the feeling from so long ago of being so sure that I was loved.  I gazed up at her and was filled with a sense of longing that she seemed to understand.  I could see her gentle eyes.  I could see her welcoming smile--the lady in the moon.

"Mama Moon," I whispered.  "Can you make things right again? Nothing feels good right now.  What can I do?"

There was no answer, just the breeze.  But I knew she had heard me.  Perhaps she would talk to me and tell me what to do soon. Perhaps when she reappeared the next month, there would be an answer.

I hurried across the parking lot to the station wagon. It was unlocked and I opened up the back door and crawled inside. It was dark but I felt around for my school satchel and found my torch in a side pocket. The beam was enough to locate an old blanket and a couple of beach towels stuffed beside the grocery bags. I lay them out and then rummaged in the bags and pulled out a packet of Eet-Sum-Mor Biscuits and a carton of orange juice that I thought should have been in the fridge hours ago. I settled in, tucking the blanket around me, and ripped open the packet of biscuits. The first bite melted in my mouth--the sweet flakiness of shortbread. Yum. Dinner and dessert tonight! I tried to slow down and chew, as Maggie insisted, but I was still so hungry. Half the packet was gone when I chugged down the orange juice. I snuggled down as best I could, gazing one last time at the glowing ball in the sky.

I muttered to myself, "I hope Peter gets us home alright. Hopefully, there are no cops about. Great dinner, Pete. I'm sure Maggie would love to know I'm getting a really healthy meal out of you and I bet Rosie will be really mad when her stew is found uneaten on the stove tomorrow. You really are a winner!"

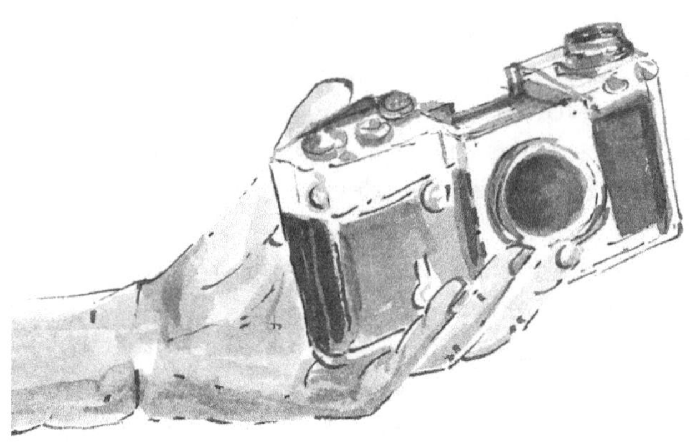

## 5. The Birthday

"Hey, China, wakey-wakey.  We've got a full day planned here. Happy birthday."  Peter stood at the door of the bedroom that I stayed in when I was with him.

It was a small bedroom but had a large window that looked out at the garden.  He had said I could use it whenever I wanted and soon after we arrived in Durban we had spent a fun morning shopping for sheets and bedcovers and even matching curtains.  We had finally chosen dark blue, with small airplanes flying through white puffy clouds.  He had also bought a wooden desk and a swivel chair that I loved to spin around.

That was the thing--it was crazy.  At times he was cool and tried to help me.  Other times, when the booze was around, he was like a chameleon.  He seemed like a different person.  He changed his mind.  He could get pretty darn angry and there were a couple of times when I got pretty scared.  Once he had threatened to take off his belt and give me a good 'lambassing.'  I can't remember what I had done or why he was so upset, but he had left me and gone through to his bedroom.  The next minute I heard him snoring away.

I sat up in bed and crossed my fingers and hoped this would be one of the good days.  Peter walked into the room and plopped down on the bed.  His curly hair was getting long, and grey I noticed, and he seemed chunkier too, even though he never seemed to eat that much, especially dinner.  He put two packages on the bed.

"Go on and open them up."  He seemed excited.

I grabbed the first box and ripped off the brown paper.  Opening it up, I forced a big smile.  "Oh wow.  That's great--a rugby shirt and ball!  Thanks a lot."

Pete smiled and ruffled my hair.  "We can go out to the park.  I think I can still manage a bit of a game."  He laughed.  "I used to play a lot you know, as a scrum-half.  You can start training and I bet a lot of your classmates would play with you."

I gave a nod, thinking to myself of my few times of playing and hating every minute.  What was the point of running around trying to get the ball to some line at the end of the field and in the process getting beaten to a pulp?  No one in my class would even want to play with me.

I grabbed the second package.  It was smaller and quite heavy.  I was curious.  I looked up at Peter who was grinning.  I ripped off the paper and gasped.  "Holy shit.  Whoops sorry.  Slipped out.  A Nikon Camera!"  Now that was really cool.

I held the camera in my hand and a distant memory flitted past.  I knew that I had seen one just like it.  I remembered the weight of it in my hands.  I remembered squinting through the lens and seeing something, something… it was a large buck with tall curving horns and I remembered the feel of another soft hand over mine, steadying the camera as I pressed the button--whirr--I let out a breath.

"Mama had a camera," I whispered.

Peter was quiet and had a faraway look on his face.  "Yes, she loved to take photos.  I thought you might like it."

"You knew my mom, right Peter?  When we lived on the farm?"

"I did Sammy."  He turned to look at me and his face was soft and he even seemed sort of sad.  "I knew her alright.  She was a very special person."

I flung myself forward and hugged him.  I never thought that I would have my own camera.  It must have cost a lot.

"Can you show me how to use it?  Can we take it with us today?  It would be great to go to the ocean and get some photos of the seagulls and stuff."

"Hey, it's your day, my boy."  He pushed himself off the bed.

"Get up now and let's have some breakfast.  Rosie has made some flapjacks.  Don't forget we are having a braai tonight.  Sure you don't want to invite anybody else besides Evan?  I know he's your friend, but he is a bit of a woos isn't he?" Peter asked as he left the room.

## 6. Good Day Gone Bad

"Now, that was a good day, Moosey," I told the battered old moose that I kept on my bed.

I gently placed my precious camera on the bedside table and dumped an armful of new clothes on the bed, half covering the stuffed toy. I was tired after our shopping trip and then the afternoon on the beach.

"I wish I could just stay in my room now. I really don't want Evan and his mom and dad over. It's been a fun birthday so far. Only wish Maggie and Bento had been here."

I lay down on the bed and closed my eyes. I could hear Rosie clanging pots in the kitchen and singing some song I couldn't understand, although the words seemed to soothe me. Oh right, she was singing in Sindebele, I realized. She had fled from Zimbabwe, too, leaving her family there and carefully saving what little money she earned to send back to them to try and ease the awful financial situation. She had told me once that we could have been neighbours when I had lived on the farm. Was that why she wanted to take care of me all the time? Had she known my mom and dad? The thought brought a wave of sadness.

How would I be celebrating my birthday if we were all still living on the farm?  An early morning hike to the dam.  We would go along the sandy trail where the African women walked balancing the heavy clay pots or metal buckets on their heads, careful to not spill a drop of the precious water.  The sun would just be peeking over the top of the trees and it would still be cool.  We would find a place under the old thorn tree and Papa would spread out his old army blanket to sit on and Mama would have the wicker basket.  We would have a thermos of hot tea sweetened with honey, and Mama would unpack the special jaffels that the cook had made.  It was if I could still smell the mouth-watering aroma and taste the crispy bacon and just-right-runny egg squishing out of the side of the toasted bread, crispy at the edges.

I would have a new fishing rod with a spinning reel that Papa had given me for my birthday.  If I was lucky, I would catch a barbel--those ugly old fish with huge whiskers that liked to slither around in the mud at the bottom of the dam.  Papa had usually helped me reel them in, but now I was ten, I bet I could get even the biggest one by myself!

Mom's friend Ruth and her kids would have made the drive from their farm in their battered old Land Rover in the afternoon.  We would have played musical chairs and everyone would get fun prizes and then the birthday cake, probably lopsided from the old wood-burning stove and covered with lumpy icing and lots of bright candles.  Mama would have taken the fresh cream that was brought in from the milking shed that morning, and made vanilla ice cream; hard as a rock from the big deep freeze, but her secret hot chocolate sauce melted it just enough to slurp it up.

* * *

"Sammy!  What the hell you been doing?  Get into the kitchen and give Rosie a hand.  I've been standing at the bloody braai cooking your meat while you laze around in your room.  Hurry it up.  Your guests are here!"  Peter's angry voice and a loud thumping on my door roused me from my daydreaming.

I bolted to a sitting position.  I could feel my throat close and I swallowed.

I heard Peter stomp down the hallway and yell, "Rosie, bring the damn ice out, now–now, and gin and tonic. I told you to get the drinks!"

"Oh please, don't let him get into one of those states tonight," I begged Moosey as I gave him a hug. I jumped off the bed and ran barefoot through the hallway and out to the back garden.

A bougainvillea hedge blocked the view of the neighbour's house. There was a small deck with a few folding chairs. A table, covered with a batik tablecloth held a bowl of potato chips, peanuts, plates, and cutlery. Some paving stones led up to a concrete slab where Peter was standing gazing down at the braai. It was made from an old forty-four-gallon drum that had been sawed in half. Metal legs had been welded to the drum. Everybody in Zimbabwe seemed to have had one just like it. The fire had burned to glowing embers. Peter flipped the long curl of Boerewors sausage and the T-bone steaks and took a chug of beer, draining the bottle. He walked to the deck and placed the bottle in a line of empties near his chair.

He turned to look at me and scowled. "Jeez, I just spent a shitload of money on buying you new clothes and you haven't even the decency to dress up a little. Go and change and get some shoes on. You're not a bloody picinini. Evan is just getting out of the car. Go on, voetsack!"

I changed quickly into my new shirt and shorts, pulled on my new tekkies and went to the kitchen. Rosie was stirring a big pot on the stove and next to it stood a steaming bowl of tomato relish.

"Ok Sam-Sam, you take out the sadza." She pulled the pot off the stove and I grabbed the handles with the potholders. It was heavy and the steam and smell from the thick, white mealie porridge wafted over me. I carried it outside and struggling to lift it, placed it on the table. Rosie followed with the bowl of sauce that added to the feast of bread rolls and baked beans. The bucket of ice, a large bottle of Gilbert's Gin and some other bottles stood on the table too. She patted me on the head and then walked back to the kitchen. She had stopped singing.

"Hi, Sammy. Happy birthday," Evan said as he came up behind me, holding a present in his hand. He had on khaki shorts and a white cotton shirt. His auburn hair had been parted on the side and slicked down with what smelled like Brylcream.

"Oh, hi Evan. Hey, thanks a lot." I took the package from him.

"I'll open it in a little bit."

I thought I had better wait to get the okay from Peter. I didn't want to do anything else wrong! I placed it on the table.

Evan's parents had made their way to join Peter at the braai. I noticed that they already had drinks in their hands. Evan's dad was a big, tall man with broad shoulders. He had a large protruding belly; a beer bop I had heard it called. He seemed to be continually upset and his face was lined with a scowl. Thin red hair was combed flat over his skull. He had on a pair of blue jean overalls and a red shirt. He looked weird. Who wore overalls these days? I had only met Evan's mom once and that was enough for me. I didn't even know her proper name, so I called her Tannie, which means Aunty in Afrikaans. She spoke English with a heavy accent and scolded Evan in a string of not-so-pretty sounding Afrikaans words that I didn't understand. She was short and dumpy with unruly greying hair and her sense of fashion was non-existent. Aunt Maggie looked like a model compared to her and wouldn't have been caught dead in the bright floral dress, gathered at the waist, with big puffy sleeves that Tannie was wearing.

Evan and I went to my bedroom so I could show him my new clothes and camera. I felt kind of bad, as I knew he got hand-me-down clothes from his cousin that were always too big for him. They never seemed to have much money--just enough for Boet to head to the pub every night. The run-down house they lived in was close to the railway station and Evan had an old bike that looked as if it had come from the dump.

We had been in the bedroom for a while and were getting hungry. The meat must have been cooked by now, I thought. It was starting to get dark outside.

"Let's go and get food." I jumped off the bed and thinking I could get some photos of my "party" to show Maggie, I grabbed the camera.

A few lights had been switched on outside and a halo of moths surrounded them. I put the camera on the far side of the table. The pile of meat had been placed close to the other food, but there was no sign of anyone having dinner. The adults were lounging in the folding chairs. The line of beer bottles near Peter's chair had lengthened. He had his favourite cut-glass tumbler in his hand. Now he was into the gin and tonic.

I handed Evan a plate.  He took the wooden spoon to the sadza, but it had turned into a thick, cold sticky mess and stuck to the spoon in big white globs.  The tomato relish was barely warm and fat had formed into gross beads on the Boerewors and steaks.

"Yuck," I said as I put the T-Bone back on the serving plate. "The bread rolls look better than that."  I spooned some baked beans onto the plate.  They would taste okay even if they were cold.

"What do you boys think you are up to?" Peter called out.

"Ummmm.  Getting food."  I answered.  "What do you think it looks like?" I mumbled.

"We aren't eating yet.  Just hold your horses!"

I sighed and slammed the plate back on the table.  "Evan is hungry.  Can't we go ahead and eat?"

"Damn it Sam.  I told you to wait.  His parents aren't ready yet."

"More like Peter is not ready yet.  I'm sorry Evan.  Let's go through to the kitchen.  I bet Rosie will give us something."

We looked at each other.  We were heading down a slippery slope and I could feel the uncomfortable knot in my stomach tighten.  We left the deck and headed inside.  I could hear the phone ringing in the hallway.  I wasn't allowed to answer it while Peter was at home and I wasn't going to bother him right now.

Rosie was standing at the kitchen sink scrubbing a large, blackened pot.  She turned and I noticed the lines on her face and a few grey curls peeking from under her doek.  She had been at the house since sunrise.

"Rosie, can we get some cheese and crackers?"  She gave a tired smile, sighed and shook her head slowly.

"Ah, maiwee," she whispered.  After going to the pantry cupboard she put out some water biscuits and a hunk of cheddar cheese, which we gobbled up in no time.

"You should go, Rosie.  It's late and you shouldn't be out in the dark."  I felt a wave of anger rush through me.

Damn Peter, making her stay here so long.  She had been on her feet all day, cleaning and cooking.  For the first time, I noticed her eyes; holding worlds of pain, and I wondered what her life must be like.

"Ah, little shamwari.  I go soon.  Baas Peter says to stay and clean up."

"Rosie, you know it's going to be ages till that happens.  We aren't even allowed to eat yet.  You look as if you are going to fall over any minute.  And you won't catch your bus if you don't go soon."

She gazed up at the clock on the wall.  It was after eight.  She sighed again.  I knew it would take her at least half an hour to walk to the bus stop, then another half an hour or more to get to the township.

"Will you go if Evan and I promise to bring everything inside? We can put stuff in the fridge and you can wash up in the morning," I pleaded.

"Oh boy, Peter is not going to like that," Evan commented.

"I really don't care what Peter likes!  It's my birthday and he is messing it up big time.  I know Maggie wouldn't want Rosie treated this way."

I turned towards her and said,  "Go on Rosie."

She hesitated again and then nodded her head.  She said nothing else, but patted me on the head and walked to the scullery, collected her coat and bag and went out the back door into the dark night.

I started trembling.  I really hadn't expected her to go.  How was I going to explain this one?  Tonight was going to be a doozy.  I sat down heavily at the kitchen table and held my head in my hands.  I could hear the phone ringing again, faint against the laughter from the deck.  It sounded as if it was coming from some distant planet.  I wanted to be on a distant planet.  I wasn't even hungry anymore.

Peter stumbled into the kitchen.  I had just glanced at the clock. It was a quarter to nine. "Right boyss, lechs eat," he slurred.  "Get Rosie to bring more ice."

"Rosie is not here."   Peter turned towards me, grasping the kitchen table to steady himself and stared at me.  His eyes were glazed.

"I told her she could go home."

Peter snorted loudly. "You bloody did not!"

"Yes, I did.  She would have missed the bus if she waited any longer."

He lurched towards me.  "You little shit.  What makes you think you can tell her when to come and go.  You paying her bloody salary? She stays till I tell her, or she can voetsak and find another job."

"Well, she is gone."  I stood up turned my back on Peter and walked towards the door.  "Do you want to eat, Evan?"

Evan looked at me, his eyes wide behind his glasses.  "I guess," he mumbled.

"Don't you turn your back on me!" I heard Peter roar as we bolted outside.

Evan's parents were piling their plates with food. There was some heated conversation between Evan and his dad and then between Tannie and Boet, but I didn't understand anything except for the 'Godverdonner.'

We found the plates we had left; the food looked even more disgusting. I knew I couldn't eat anything, but Evan took his to a seat on the far side of the deck and sat face down, picking at his food. I stood there. I couldn't move. What should I do? Could I just go and hide in my room?

I picked up my camera and without even thinking, started taking some photos--the couple shovelling food as if they hadn't eaten for a week--the boy hunched over, hugging his arms and staring into the distance. I spun around and pressed, capturing Peter as he swayed towards me. I brought the camera down and swallowed. My chest felt as if it was being squished into a hard ball. I had never seen his face like that before.

He was snarling and his eyes were those of a devil man; focused on me! He came towards me and gripped my forearms. I could feel the squeeze of his hands and flinched. He started to shake me. My legs felt weak and I was getting dizzy from the rattle-rattle of my body as he emphasized every word with a harder push.

"I'll teach you to walk away, you disrespectful brat!"

My fingers were getting numb and I could feel the camera slipping from my grasp. No, no. I pushed forward with all my strength and felt Peter falter. I groaned and gave another thrust. Peter tottered backward releasing my arms, as the camera slid from my grasp. I collapsed forward on my knees onto the small patch of lawn as the camera landed on the soft grass.

"Hey. This food is lekker. Get some grub," Boet called out.

Peter straightened himself and paused, a bewildered look on his face. Slowly he turned towards the guests.

He gave a wave of his hand. "Ja, I will be with you, soon as I bring us another round."

I kept kneeling on the ground and folded myself into a ball. I was breathing heavily and cradling the camera. My eyes were closed. I wanted to disappear into the earth. Had Peter forgotten about me? I sent silent thanks to Boet for calling out and saving me, for now at least. I heard the tinkling of ice and glasses and heard footsteps on the deck walking past me. Voices and laughter floated over me, but I stayed where I was.

"Sammy?" Evan had crept up to me and was tapping me on the shoulder. "You alright?"

I opened my eyes and saw him squatting in front of me, a tear sliding down his cheek.

"I'm okay. Here give me a hand." My voice was shaking.

He stood up, put out a scrawny arm and helped haul me up.

"Dammit. He is acting so crazy. Don't worry Evan. Let's just leave them to it and keep out of the way. I'm going to take the food inside. They will only be interested in the drinks from now on."

We took some time clearing away the food and taking it inside. I wasn't really sure what to do with it all, but between Evan and I, we found some Tupperware containers to put the leftovers in and stacked the dirty dishes and pots in the sink. Poor Rosie had work piling up already. Evan had taken the food to the fridge and shoved it in.

"Hey look," he said with a happy laugh. "I found a surprise." On the second shelf of the fridge was a chocolate cake. 'Hapy Day to Sam-Sam' had been written in icing on it.

"Aw, Rosie must have baked it this morning. She doesn't know how to spell," I laughed.

We pulled the cake onto the kitchen table and after finding a knife, cut into the gooey chocolate. The first bite was delicious and we grinned at each other. This was the best part of the evening! It didn't matter that there wasn't a candle or a happy birthday song.

I was cutting a second slice for each of us when Evan's dad appeared in the doorway. "Let's go," is all he said.

Evan scrunched up his face and mouthed, "Sorry!"

He stood up right away leaving the last bite of his cake and walked to the door, ducking away from his dad. They disappeared through the garden. I knew I should go out and say goodbye but I just sat at the table, looking at my birthday treat and feeling a wave of bitterness flood through me.

I heard the car doors slam and the engine rev and then a squeal of tyres as they pulled away. I sat there for a few more minutes. A crash from outside startled me. I did not want to go see what it was.

I had done what I could to help Rosie. Peter could clean up his own damn mess! I heard a yell and a string of cuss words and then I knew I was in trouble when a form staggered to the doorway.

The next few minutes were a blur to me. Peter lunged himself at me, yelling about manners, insolence, eating the bloody cake and being ungrateful, and then giving me a bloody clap around the ears. He had the camera in his hand and was waving it in the air. The yelling continued. Did I ask permission to take his goddamn picture? Who was I going to show them to? What was I trying to prove? I just stood there, wondering what had happened to my great birthday. He lifted the camera high in the air and told me there would be no pictures of this party and I saw his arm swing back.

I ran forward, jumping up and as I couldn't reach high enough, I slammed into his stomach. With a loud groan, he bent over and the hand holding the camera came down. I wrestled it out of his hands. I spun around and started to run down the hallway towards my bedroom. As I turned to look back, I saw he had pulled the leather belt from his trousers and was coming towards me, waving it in the air. I knew he was still cussing and yelling but the pounding in my ears was all I could hear. I had to make it to the bedroom. I had to lock the door before he could get me!

I stumbled and he came closer and closer. The end of the belt flicked down and just reached my shin. A sharp pain ricocheted upwards. I barely reached my door, pushed it open and went into the room and then turning and thrusting my weight against it, tried to close it. I could feel Peter's weight holding it in place. Frantically I looked at the handle. There was no way I was going to be able to hold the door shut and turn the lock on the doorknob. I had to get away. I stepped back from the door and as it swung back, he stumbled forward into the room.

"Leave me alone!" I yelled and wormed my way past him, sprinting down the hall for the front door.

I could feel the stinging on my shin where the leather belt had cut in and I could feel the burning in my eyes. I had just made it to the front door when it flew open. I careened forward almost crashing into the person standing there. I turned to look behind me. Peter was pounding down the hall, the belt still flailing in his hands. He didn't seem to notice that I had stopped or that someone was blocking the door.

"You little shit. Just you wait. I'll beat the living daylights out of you."

I froze and then as if waking up from an awful nightmare, I saw the person in the doorway. "Maggie. Move away. Don't let him hurt you."

My aunt stood there. Her face was pale and her eyes wide with shock. She folded me into her arms. "Oh my God, Sammy. What's going on? I've been trying to call all day. We had delays but we wanted to get back for your birthday."

As he came closer to us, Peter stumbled and then shaking his head slowed to a walk.

He looked at Maggie then stopped. "What you doing here?" he slurred. "Get out of the way. That boy needs to learn some manners." He picked up his belt again and waved it in the air.

Maggie ducked.

"You get away," I yelled and freed myself from Maggie's hug.

I pushed forward and rammed myself at Peter. He gripped me around the waist and we wrestled together. He started to swat me around the ears and I knew I wasn't going to be able to hold him back. The burn of anger rose higher as I pounded my fists into his belly. A ringing blow caught me off guard and as I fell sideways to the floor, another figure appeared at the doorway.

I lay curled on the floor but could just see a tall, well-built man move swiftly into the hall. There was a crack of fist meeting jaw and Peter went tumbling back. He fell down and lay there, as still as could be. I looked up. I felt a rush of relief, as I saw Bento was kneeling over him.

"He is passed out. Let him sleep it off on the hall mat, like the dog he is," Bento said, rubbing his fist.

I couldn't believe he was there. He looked like the perfect hero-- swarthy skin, curly dark hair and penetrating eyes. He gave me a slight smile and picked me up in his strong arms. He held me tightly, rocking me and talking quietly to me. I buried my head in his shoulder.

"What a brave fellow you are, protecting our Maggie like that." His familiar Portuguese accent comforted me.

"Sammy, come with me and let's pack your suitcase," Maggie said. Her voice was all choked up.

Bento gave me another squeeze and then lowered me down.

Maggie and Bento glanced at each other.  He nodded his head and blew her a kiss.  She closed her eyes for a moment and took in a breath, then walked towards me and took me firmly by the hand.  She led me quickly toward my room.

"Get all your things Sam," I heard Bento call out.  "You won't be staying here again, meu amigo."

## 7. Sanctuary

When I woke up, I could feel the warmth of the sun on my face. It felt so good. I kept my eyes closed and burrowed down under the soft, cosy eiderdown. It was quiet. All I could hear was my breathing and the soft tick–tick of the grandfather clock in the hall. I must have fallen back to sleep. The sound of beautiful music wafted over me. Where was I? I remembered Maggie tucking me into the small couch and kissing me on the cheek. Then, I remembered the horrible ending to my birthday. I curled up again and rubbed my shin. It felt pretty sore and swollen. I didn't want to get up.

A deep voice booming from the kitchen started to sing echoing the trilling of a woman's song, and I smiled. Bento must be playing his special record again. I was beginning to learn some of the Portuguese words. A delicious smell drifted from the kitchen and my stomach grumbled--I was hungry. I opened my eyes and looked around the study. It was painted in a soft blue colour like the sky. I liked this room. Bento had so many books on shelves and beautiful pictures on the walls. I especially liked the painting he had above his big wooden desk. It was of a man standing with a badza in his hand like the Africans used on the farm. He had a book in the other hand.

Whenever I looked at him, I felt that I somehow knew him.

The couch was tucked underneath a large window. Usually, heavy curtains were covering the window. They had large colourful birds flying in and out of beautiful, tall green trees, but someone must have pulled them back and the morning sun poured in. Across the room was a big, red leather chair tucked into the corner. It was smooth and the leather was almost shiny. It sat on a cosy patterned carpet. I had spent lots of time curled up in the chair reading while Bento was at his desk.

As I climbed off the couch I found that my slippers and dressing gown had been unpacked and put by the chair and yes, my camera was there and it looked as if it wasn't broken at all; the only good thing about yesterday. I opened the door and was about to step out when I heard Maggie's voice.

"No, Peter. There is no way he is going to come back. I know you are sorry, but it's just not going to happen. We need to have a chat, but right now I suggest that you start looking at places that you can go to. You need to get some help. There is a residential centre just outside of town. I can look into different programs if you want my help."

I peeked my head around the door. She was standing in the hallway with her back to me. The side table against the wall held a vase of flowers and the telephone. Maggie's face was reflected in the large mirror that hung above the table.

She was frowning as she held the receiver in her hand. "No. No. That is my decision. I have full custody of him. So don't even think of trying to go down that road. You know jolly well you don't stand a chance with your history. Oh, and I've sent our gardener over to your house to tell Rosie to come here. You will have to find someone else. She is going to work for us now and stay on the property." Another long silence. "I'm the one that sent her to you. Her family was living on the Nata reserve. She doesn't have to put up with your nonsense."

She took a big breath and shook her head. "Yes, she is to come over right away. You can deal with the chaos you have created. I have to go. Goodbye."

* * *

The day after my birthday was better than my actual birthday. Bento had made waffles with syrup and strawberries. We ate together at the dining room table that Maggie had decorated with cloth placemats and napkins, and we even used the sparkling silver knives and forks that were usually only used at Christmas. There was fresh orange juice in a crystal jug that Maggie had somehow brought to South Africa, and then special chocolate that they had brought back from Portugal.

The presents were cool too--a whole tray of beautiful paints, a big sketchbook, and some fun board games. Then the big surprise--a guitar! It was just the right size for me to get my fingers around the neck; the ones at school were just too big and made it very hard to try to learn the chords. It was a deep reddish colour and had a pattern of shimmering swirls on the neck and body; mother-of-pearl, Maggie said. I had learned how to tune the instruments at our after-school classes, and boy did this sound good when I strummed it.

We went to a movie and had popcorn with extra butter. At the park, I had a climbing competition with Bento in the big jacaranda tree and Maggie even went on the swings with me, though she didn't go that high. We had dinner at the Chinese restaurant where old Mr Wong brought a special sticky rice cake and Maggie brought a chocolate cupcake with a candle in it. I knew that wasn't Chinese.

As I was getting ready for bed after a hot bath, I wondered how Evan was doing. I wouldn't see him for a while, as we had a break from school and I wouldn't be seeing him now at the pub. Maggie had told me that I was going to stay with her and Bento fulltime and I was glad about that, but I wished I could have Evan come and live with us or help him out. I hated to think of him having to put up with Tannie and Boet.

Maggie came to tuck me in; I was pretty old for that now that I was ten, but I knew she liked to say goodnight. "Is it okay to sleep in the study for a while Sammy? I'm going to fix up the room off the back patio if you think you would like that. I figured now you are older you wouldn't mind being in there."

"It's fine, Maggie. That would be cool to have for a bedroom and I like this room too." I gazed around. "Who is that man in the painting there?" I pointed over to Bento's desk.

Maggie smiled. "I must have told you about him."

I shook my head.

"Are you sure?  Well, this can be your bedtime story," she said as she sat on the side of the bed.

"There was once a young man who lived in England.  He loved to read and would spend hours in his tiny bedroom, learning about the adventures of people who had travelled far away to different parts of the world.  The stories he liked best were the ones of men who had crossed the ocean and sailed to Africa like Doctor David Livingstone and Henry Morton-Stanley.  He decided that he too would go there.  When he was nineteen years old he boarded a ship leaving his home, family, and sweetheart, and off he went.  After a long, long journey, which wasn't very pleasant because he got very seasick and had mostly yucky food like cabbage to eat, he arrived in Cape Town."

"Cape Town at the end of South Africa?" I asked.

Maggie nodded.  "He had to travel a long way still, as he had joined the Methodist Church and they wanted him to go, guess where?"

I shook my head and shrugged my shoulders.

"They wanted him to go to Zimbabwe.  Well, it was called Southern Rhodesia then.  He travelled by train from Cape Town.  There were just steam trains at that time and it was all very different for him.  He wasn't used to the heat and flies and well, lots of other things.  I'm sure he wondered if he had made a big mistake, especially when he found out that he was going to have to travel by donkey cart from Plumtree."

"The Plumtree Mama and I went to sometimes?"  I had a hazy memory of shops and an old hotel.

Maggie smiled softly and nodded.  "Well, the journey from Plumtree was even worse for him.  The donkey was old, with a dirty, shaggy coat that attracted the flies.  It was very, very slow.  There was an African man who drove the cart.  He was a big, tall man with a mean-looking scar on his cheek, so he looked very frightening.  Of course, the man was a Matabele and he spoke Sindebele, which the Englishman couldn't understand at all."

"I still remember some Sindebele.  Bongo means thank you and the doves were called ijuba," I said.  "Do you remember any, Maggie?"

"Hmm, no I never really learned it.  I was living in Mashonaland and they speak Shona there.  Well, the cart hit a big old bump in the road and one of the wheels fell off.  While the Matabele man was fixing it, the poor Englishman was attacked by a baby warthog!"

"How could he be attacked by a baby warthog?" I laughed.

Maggie laughed too. "Well remember, this young man had never seen any African animals before and was really scared when the warthog came charging towards him. You must admit a warthog is a pretty strange looking beast!"

"I know they are ugly," I chuckled again, "with the tusks and silly tail that always stands straight up, but it was only a baby, right?"

"Ja, so the African man had a jolly good laugh, too. Anyway, they eventually got to the Nata Reserve and the Mission."

She paused. "Yes, the Nata reserve and the Mission station, where you and Mama spent so much time, and where I came to get you." She was silent for quite a long time. "After a while, the man learned to live in the bush, with the heat and the flies."

"And the spiders and Christmas beetles that stick in your hair if you don't sleep with a mosquito net and the whining mosquitos, bzzzzzzzzzz, that get through the net. And the snakes and the muddy water from the dam and the big thunderstorms and the…" I added.

"Oh Sammy, it's not that awful, is it? Living in Africa?" She grinned.

"Did he love anything about Africa?" I asked.

"Oh yes. He learned to love the big sky and camping in the bush and the herds of antelope. As you can see in the picture, he loved the land and growing mealies and, gosh, he loved it so much that he lived in Africa for the rest of his life."

"Was he a real man? Or is it just a story?"

She nodded again. "He was real alright."

"Do you know what his name was?" I asked with a yawn.

"I do. His name was Morris." She smiled at my look of surprise.

"Like my name?"

"And mine," she said. "Can you guess who he was?"

"I'm not sure."

"He was my grandfather and your great-grandfather Simon Morris."

"Well, okay." I paused. I know my face had scrunched up the way it always did when I was trying to figure out an arithmetic problem or something. "But, if he was OUR family, why is his picture hanging in Bento's study? Did you bring it with you?"

Maggie stood up, shaking her head.  She bent over and gave me a kiss on the cheek.  She tucked the eiderdown around me.  Her face was soft and she smiled again.

"It's late and that, Sammy, is another whole story, which will have to wait for another night."

## 8. A Change in the Air
## One Year Later

It was on my eleventh birthday that I found out my life was about to change.  It had been a great day!  We had a fun time at the skating rink with Maggie and Bento and I had even taken a couple of new friends from school.  Evan had come too.  I didn't see him very much now and he was really quiet.  I noticed he had a bruise on his face.  I asked him about it, but he just shrugged and didn't say anything.

That night Maggie had come through to my room.  She had knocked on the door.  "Can I come in?"

"Sure, I'm awake.  What's up?"

"Did you have a good time today?"  She perched on the edge of the bed.

Her hair was glowing in the lamplight; it looked like rose gold and it had grown longer so it fell about her face.  The memory of my Mama's hair falling softly down in a golden waterfall flickered past.  It had been so long since I had last seen her and Papa.  It was strange how the memories seemed to drift in at the most unexpected times and mesh around my heart; a cocoon of feelings, flashes of faces and landscapes; whispers of love that seemed to vibrate with the same intensity that they had five years ago.

I looked over at the one photograph of my parents that I kept on my dresser. It was in a dark wooden frame that had been hand-carved. I knew the name of the waterfall that flowed down the side of the frame. The Africans called it Mosi-Oa-Tunya--The Smoke That Thunders. All the tourists called it Victoria Falls.

There were two people in the photo--Mama with long, shiny blond hair and a sweet smile on her face. Papa had his arm around her. He was tall, with short, dark hair and his face was looking down at a baby--it was me!

"Sammy? You tired? I can talk to you tomorrow if you like."

"Oh, sorry Maggie. I was daydreaming I guess. I'm okay."

She took a breath. "What do you think of moving to America?"

I didn't say anything.

She waited for a while before she said, "You know we can't go back to Zimbabwe. The country is still in so much turmoil. We wouldn't want to go back to that."

Our eyes locked for a moment.

"South Africa is heading the same way."

She paused again and I swear I could hear her heartbeat. Domp, domp, domp!

"Bento's dad lives in California and we can get permission to live there." She smiled. "After Bento and I get married."

"You guys are getting married? That's cool."

Maggie blushed.

"Can I go with you?" My voice quivered a little. There was no way I was going to go back to being with Peter.

"Of course. Sammy, I would never have considered it if you could not come. I have custody of you. That basically means you are my kid. And Bento would be your step-dad." She leaned forward and touched my shoulder. "I know it will be a big change, but I think perhaps living in a new place would be good, for all of us. A fresh start."

* * *


Maggie didn't know I was back from school early. I bet she had forgotten that we had a half-day because of exams starting tomorrow.

I wasn't trying to sneak around and hear their conversation. I had just gone through to my room when I heard voices in the hall. She walked through to the kitchen and sat down at the table, with Peter following behind her. When I saw him, I didn't move from my desk, the study sheets for my science forgotten. Through the door that I had left slightly open I could see the back of Maggie's head and just hear what they were saying.

"Damn you, Maggie, you have no right to just drag him off to another continent. You think you can always get your way? I have a say in this too, you know."

"Oh, no Peter. Not now. Not with what has happened this last year. I've finally realized why Shelly couldn't be with you and married James Dupree. My sister knew what would happen with this problem of yours."

She had taken a big breath in and I could see the back of her head moving from side to side.

"I had no idea that things were so bad Pete. Why didn't you talk to me? Ask for some help?"

Peter snorted. "Oh God, Maggie don't be so dramatic! Everybody goes to the pub. I can name a dozen people that have had fender benders or been acting like idiots or yelling at the kids after a couple of chiboolies. If I'm an alcoholic, then three-quarters of the people living in Zim and S.A. are too."

She was quiet for a while and spoke softly, so I had to listen carefully to hear. "You really think that is okay? You think you can go on living like this, without dealing with the consequences of what you do? You're a smart guy and I know you care for Sammy. Can't you see how this has affected your life already?"

"Well, excuse me, Miss High and Mighty. What do you think I was doing in that God-forsaken treatment centre for so many weeks? Having a fun holiday? It's all cool now. I'm able to leave that crazy place for time off and I'll be signed out in another two weeks. I'll be at home before you leave Africa, and I want to have the boy around."

I shifted in my seat and the chair scraped against the wooden floor. I gulped. Had they heard me? I was so thirsty but I wasn't going to take the chance of getting a cool drink from my satchel behind the door. I wanted to hear what else they had to say.

"I know things are okay for now," Maggie said, "but Shelly decided to give Sammy a stable childhood. She hoped the corruption in Zimbabwe would end; she had at least tried to give him some sort of normal, loving upbringing before they were murdered."

"Yeah, and it was her stupid decision to be with James and to stay on the Nata Reserve!" Peter thumped the table. "If she had been with me in Bulawayo she would probably be alive still."

There was a long, long silence.

"I told you when you first got Sammy that I would help and I have, you can't deny that. I don't want to fight you Maggie, but I have every right to have a say in his upbringing."

"Actually, Peter, you don't. There is no written documentation of any kind claiming you as having any rights and I have been given sole custody of Sammy. There is no legal way that you can prove anything. It would just add to more hurt and heartache to go down that road. As it is, we can still try to make the best of it. You can see him when it works out and we won't cut off ties completely."

Peter stood up and ran a hand through his hair. Then, pointed his finger at Maggie and leaning over the table, he waved it around, close to her face.

"You know what? I think I'll just go over to the school right now, and tell him the truth. He is not a baby anymore. Why shouldn't he know? We should have done that a long time ago." He turned to walk to the door. "Yup, I think its bloody time!"

Maggie stood up quickly and ran around to stand right in front of him. I was still peeking through the door, scrunched down in my chair. I couldn't believe they hadn't noticed that my door was open.

"Don't you dare! He has had enough to cope with this last little while and now with the move, it's not the right time. He needs to hold onto the memories of Shelly and James. It hasn't been that long. I promise if you do, there will be hell to pay!" Maggie exclaimed.

"Oh, ja. What you going to do?" Pete had marched over and stood right in front of Maggie.

"Peter, I don't want to fight with you. I appreciate all you have done and I know things haven't been easy for you either. Let's not go down some road we will both regret. There has been enough heartbreak for everybody. Let's honour Shelly and keep working together to give Sammy what he needs."

Peter glared at her. "I know Bento will be a good step-dad but he needs me too."

"Don't you do anything right now!  Sammy needs you to keep yourself on track, so he has respect for you again."  Maggie turned towards the hallway, ushering Peter with a wave of her hand.  "If you do say anything, that rather large loan that Bento gave you to keep you out of court will be quickly called in, I promise you that!"

## 9. Forging a Relationship

"Hi. Who are you here to see?" The lady in the starched blue dress glanced up from behind the white counter. She smiled.

"Peter Nell. Is he in his room?" I asked.

"Yes, you can go ahead. Is he your uncle?"

"No. But I used to call him Uncle Peter when I was younger."

"You look like you could have some family traits," she laughed. She reached over the counter and patted down the cowlick in my hair.

I hated that stupid wave, and what a dumb name--COWLICK! Yuck. I took a step away from her and I tried to flatten down the front of my hair.

I hurried down the passage and made my way towards the far end of the building. It wasn't a hospital but it sort of smelled like one and had the same slick, shiny floors. I had been here before. It must have been a year ago just after my tenth birthday. Peter had stayed here for some time. Maggie said that he had gotten very stressed and had to take a break in this residential home. I didn't believe that story, especially after what I had heard a few days ago. What did he have to get stressed about?  He didn't seem to have a job anymore and was always just hanging around with the chaps at the clubs.

When he had gone back home, after being released from the centre, I had even visited him a couple of times by myself.  We had gone to the movies and the beach and he had been pretty cool.  He didn't yell at me, or anything and said he was sorry about my birthday and being so cranky and he was trying to sort himself out.  Good for him!  But I was so glad I didn't have to see him all the time.

It had been a while now since Maggie and I had given up our little flat and had moved in with Bento.  They fixed up my bedroom and I had started at a new school that I liked much better.  I did lots of afternoon activities; they even had photography and guitar classes and I joined the tennis club.  Rosie was working for us and she and I spent time together if Maggie and Bento were out.

Then it had happened again.  Another accident!  Peter's car was totalled.  He busted up his head.  The police showed up one afternoon to talk to Maggie.  I guess he had been having one of his crazy nights drinking again.  Now he was back in 'The Jacaranda Centre.'

I didn't really want to visit him, but Maggie thought I should see him a few times before we left Africa.

"After all," she had said, "he did help us a lot when we first came here and he is very fond of you.  He will miss you a lot, Sammy."

Right!  He never did think of me much when he was hanging out at the country club.  I would make this a really quick visit.

Peter turned towards me as I went into his room.  He was sitting on a twin bed.  There was a small side table, with a water flask and a few books.  An uncomfortable looking chair and a small coffee table were in the corner.  There was only one window that opened onto a drab courtyard.  It didn't feel like a great place to hang out.

I got quite a shock when I saw him.  He had a bandage over one side of his head and I could see a bruise spreading down his cheek.  His hair had been shaved on that one side so he looked all lop-sided.  He sat and looked at me for a while.  He seemed sad.

He got up from the bed and hobbled towards me like an old, old man.  "Hey, Sammy.  I'm quite a sight, aren't I?"  He gave a half-hearted laugh.

"Here."  I thrust a round cake tin towards him.  "Rosie baked you some banana bread and biscuits."

"Oh, that's lekker. Say thank you for me. She doing okay?"

A lot better than you, I thought. "Ja, she's fine. She is happy that she is living on the property. Saves her the bus ride."

We both stared at each other. I wanted him to know that I had heard him talking to Maggie, but I was kind of scared. I didn't want to have him yelling and getting mad at me again.

"Did Maggie tell you we were going to move to California?"

Peter made his way to the chair and sat down slowly. He pointed to the corner of the room. "Grab that folding chair."

I picked up the chair and opened it up. I put it a little distance away and perched on the edge.

"Kind of a crazy move, don't you think? Hightailing it to America? Maggie might want to go with Bento, but I bet you don't really want to leave Africa, right?"

He was speaking quietly and he seemed so, I don't know, like a balloon that had been pricked and all the air was coming out-- shhhhhhhh. He gazed at me with this weird kind of expression on his face. I hadn't ever seen him like this. I didn't know who this guy was.

I shrugged my shoulders. "I don't really mind. It might be pretty interesting and Maggie says we will come back to visit."

"You know Maggie and Bento are going to be gadding around and starting a new life. They'll be kind of busy. They may not have much time to take care of you." He scrunched back into the chair and rubbed his arm. I hadn't noticed the bandage on his forearm.

There was a very long pause. Was he waiting for me to answer? I could hear the rattle of metal carts in the passage and the hooting of a car horn outside.

"I'll be out of here next week and I have things all sorted out now." Peter moved forward to the front of the chair and sat up straighter.

I saw the expression on his face change and he went all rigid around his mouth. "You know Sam, I bet your mom wouldn't have wanted you to be gapping it from Africa. You were born here. If Maggie hadn't met Bento she would be staying in Africa too. You don't have to go trailing after her you know. You can always stay here with me."

I bit my lip. "You didn't know my mom so well. She would have wanted me to be with Maggie. That's her sister after all!" I snapped back. "And you know, we already have the tickets and visas and stuff. They arrived last week." I wriggled around in my chair.

"Well, I did know your mom, better than you think." He stared straight at me. "She would never have left."

I could see him clenching his fists and his brow started to furrow the way it did when he was getting riled up. "I think it's a bad choice, but nobody seems to give a damn about my opinion."

"I bet we will visit before too long. Bento loves Africa too, and he says he'll still do some of his art classes at the university sometimes. So we will see you." I felt as if I had this smile kind of plastered over my face. I had to get out of there.

"Hey," I said standing up and refolding the chair. "I've got a class I have to go to. The teacher is pretty cranky, so I better not be late." I set the chair back in the corner. "I'll see you again before we leave, for sure, okay?"

Peter just gazed at me for a long time and then nodded. Jeez, why did I feel so bad? He was the one who had been the idiot, but I was glad he was getting out of this place and his head would be better soon. He would be okay.

"Alright. Bye then." I waved as I walked towards the door, then stopped and turned around. "Hey, if you need anything when you get home, I could help if you want. You know any errands or anything."

I closed the door behind me and hurried down the hall and slipped past the blond lady at the desk. You're the idiot, Sammy. I hope he doesn't take me up on that offer, I thought, as I sprinted out of the building and ran towards the park. My class didn't start for half an hour. I had escaped into the fresh air and bright African sunshine.

## 10. The Grand Finale

I knew I would never forgive Peter for what had happened. The devil man had returned and I hated him. I never wanted to see him again. I could not be his friend ever again.

Things had been going so well and we were so close to leaving. A few more days and we would be boarding the plane and off to a new life. The house was packed up and some things shipped off to California. Lots of stuff had been sold and given away to the thrift store. I had a big new suitcase with wheels. I had stuffed it full, and could just barely close it when I sat on it. The last-minute clothes would fit into the matching carry-on case; it had wheels too.

I hadn't minded when Peter had telephoned Maggie to ask if he could take me up on my offer to help him. He wanted to fix up the little rockery in the side yard. He said he could use a strong eleven-year-old to help him out. He had been back at home for a few weeks and I had seen him a couple of times when Maggie had dropped off a casserole and then some groceries. He seemed to be pretty happy.

That day, Maggie dropped me off and went to do some errands and last minute travel plans. I was pleased with what we did. It was hard work and I seemed to do most of it, as Peter was still slow going.  I moved a bunch of rocks and we filled in the spaces with succulents and other plants.  By lunchtime, I was done.

It had turned out to be a hot day and we were both hungry.  There didn't seem to be much in the house, so Peter decided we would just swing by the country club and pick up a couple of bacon and egg rolls.  That's when I began to get that sinking feeling again.  Maggie had told me that Peter was on a health kick and would be watching what he ate and was not going to be drinking anymore.  I wondered why she didn't just come out and say it.  Peter drank too much and his 'sorting himself out' a year ago hadn't worked, so he had ended up back in the Centre.  My friend at school knew about the Jacaranda Centre--a place where his uncle had gone because he was an alcoholic.  Did Maggie think I didn't know what was going on?

I wasn't going to let Peter get away with anything anymore so I said, "Let's just make some peanut butter sandwiches.  Maggie should be back to pick me up soon.  We still have stuff to do, so I don't want to keep her waiting."

"Can't stand peanut butter and we could both use a nice cold drink.  Turned out to be a bloody hot day.  We'll just grab the food and come right home.  Come on.  How about some chips and ice cream, too?  My last treat for you," Peter said.

We drove over in the jalopy of a car that Peter had just bought from his golf buddy.  His old car had been totalled in his last accident.  The club was very busy that day and I went to the small counter near the pro shop to order the food.  Peter said he would pop into the bar, just for a moment, to see if his friend was there with the car registration papers.  I waited outside under the large flamboyant tree watching the players tee off.  After about fifteen minutes I heard my name called and collected the rolls, two bags of chips, two Cokes, and a carton of chocolate ice cream.  I hurried back to the bar.  The ice cream wasn't going to take long to melt.

It was it if I had been thrown back into a horrible picture from the past.  Peter sat at the bar.  Next to him was Boet.  In the corner in the old armchair was Evan.  Taller and lanky, his red hair a little longer and new glasses, but still playing cards and waiting, waiting.

I waved at him but did not go over.  I had to get Peter out of there.  I came up behind the bar, hoping that somehow things would be okay, but then I saw the glass of Coke, only a few sips drunk from it, had been pushed aside and the Castle Lager was in Peter's hand. What the hell was he doing?

"Peter I've got the food. We have to go. Maggie will be waiting."

"Hold your horses. I'll be with you in a sec. Haven't seen Boet for ages. Go and say hi to Evan."

"No. We have to go. You shouldn't be here. You know that."

He turned to look at me and I knew then, that whatever good had come from him being sober, had evaporated in that rank and dim atmosphere with the first sip of the cold, life-quenching alcoholic drink. I had no power to change his mind. I could feel the burn in my stomach and this fire of anger starting to sweep through me. I wasn't going to wait for the disastrous outcome. I was through putting up with his bullshit. He hadn't changed a bit.

With fists clenched, I stormed to the end of the counter and called out to Phineas who was behind the bar. "Hi, Phineas. I need to use the phone."

He nodded and he led me back towards the phone hanging on the wall. "You okay, Sam? Things better now? You getting big, hey? He laughed.

"Yes, but I'll be saying goodbye. I'm leaving South Africa soon. You take care of yourself okay?" My voice was all crackly.

He smiled and then hurried back to the far end of the counter where a group of men had seated themselves.

I called Maggie. I went outside and I waited in the car park. It only took her ten minutes to drive up. She had me wait in the car while she went into the bar. I told her I wanted to go with her. She yelled at me to wait in the car. That was the first time I heard Maggie get really cross with me. When she came out she was pale and had tears in her eyes. Her hands shook as she drove away.

"Maggie I know he shouldn't be drinking again and that is why he crashed his car and ended up back at that treatment place. It's just as well we are going away. I know he is your friend, but I really don't want to see him again."

She didn't say anything.

"He really has a problem, doesn't he?" I turned to look at her.

She nodded and in a very quiet voice said, "Yes, Sammy. He does have a problem which, I'm afraid, we can't solve for him."

* * *

The call came just after midnight. I heard the muffled ring-ring, ring-ring, and by the time I had woken up, Bento had answered the call and Maggie was standing as still as a granite kopje next to him. I pulled on my dressing gown and slippers and stumbled into the hall. A grim-faced Bento caught my eye.

"Yes, yes. And the boy? Oh, I'm sorry, sorry." He shook his head. "Yes, of course. Thank you." He put down the telephone receiver carefully.

Bento and Maggie called Rosie from her kia and asked her to stay in the house with me, although I told them I was fine by myself. They had to go to the hospital. Peter had, not to my surprise, been in another accident. He had other people in the car. 'The boy,' Bento had said, and I knew with a sinking heart, that something had happened to Evan. I couldn't get back to sleep. I should have kept in contact with Evan. I should have asked Maggie and Bento to check in on him. I hadn't been a very good friend. It was a long night. Eventually, I did drift off to sleep.

Maggie and Bento returned around lunchtime. I knew things weren't good by the look on Maggie's face. We sat down at the kitchen table. We were going to delay our trip for a week. She had already called the airline.

Peter, Boet, and, of course, poor Evan had been at the Club until about eleven o'clock that night. When Boet had tried to start his car the battery was dead. Peter was going to give them a ride home. Yes, he was drunk and should not have been driving. They had hit the curb at the roundabout near the shopping centre, bounced off and as he pulled back onto the road, had not looked for oncoming traffic. A grocery truck had admittedly been going pretty fast and had no time to stop before it ploughed into the car. It had flipped it over and even seemed to drag it for some distance. The truck driver had pulled off and help had been called. By the time the ambulance and police had arrived and managed to get the passengers out of the car, one was dead and two injured.

I held my breath waiting for Maggie to continue, but she had stopped talking and was quietly crying. One dead, two injured. Who? Bento had walked behind her and placed his hands on her shoulders. It must be Peter. She took out a tissue from her handbag and blew her nose.

"Sammy, Peter is okay. He has a broken arm and opened up his wound again." Her head shook, as if in disbelief.

"Evan?" I whispered.

"It was Boet who died. Evan is alive but he has an awful injury." Her voice cracked. "Oh, God. He has lost his leg and the other is badly mangled. They are doing what they can to save it."

I remember the words sort of floating above me. Trying to save it. Could that mean he wouldn't have any legs? My brain couldn't seem to figure it out. Bento had sat back down, running his hands through his hair and we all just sat there. My fist crashed onto the table. I jumped up.

"It's Peter's fault. He should be the one who's dead! What's going to happen to Evan?" I had to get away. I pushed the chair back and it went clattering to the floor.

I ran out of the house and into the back yard. The tall, old avocado tree beckoned to me and I climbed up as high as I could. The breeze seemed to caress me as if to dry the moisture on my cheeks. I could hear the soothing, familiar sound of a mourning dove in the branches that reached above me. I closed my eyes and held onto those strong limbs, praying for--I didn't know what. I didn't understand.

The mourning dove stopped its call and with wings ruffling, took flight higher and higher into the huge sky. I watched it until it was just a blur far, far away. I wanted to fly far, far away too. My life seemed to be full of twists and turns and loops and steep plunges. I decided that I didn't really like this roller coaster ride very much.

## 11. Friends Fly In

California was cool!  My mind was kind of boggled though.  We seemed to have travelled for days.  We drove about 300 kilometres from Durban to Johannesburg, and then caught the Jumbo Jet to London.  We had a stopover, but had to stay at the airport; Heathrow I think it was.  I was disappointed, as I wanted to explore and go and see the Queen or something.  From there we flew for hours and hours to Los Angeles.  I had slept pretty well and had lots of meals at weird times and watched loads of movies on these small T.V. screens.

Wow, it was crazy at Los Angeles International Airport!  I had never seen so many people in different kinds of clothing--saris, turbans, and shawls, and speaking so many different languages.  We found that all our suitcases had arrived, which Bento said was a miracle.  Then after customs and immigration, we were squished along with this stream of people through to the exit gate.  The crowds waiting were holding up signs and yelling, crying, hugging, and juggling bunches of flowers and balloons.  Maggie grabbed my hand and wouldn't let go.

We pushed our way towards the exit sign and then a tall man with longish, grey hair yelled out at Bento, waving like crazy and coming towards us.

"Pai. Oi," Bento called back, then rushed forward to meet him. They gave each other a big hug. "This is my father, Jeffrey." He smiled broadly. "Or you can call him Avo if you like, Sam. That means Grandfather in Portuguese."

Maggie and I were wrapped in a hug too, and then we made our way outside to the car park. Somehow we managed to load everything into his V. W. Kombi van and Maggie and I settled onto the back seat. I just about had a fit when he took off.

"We're on the wrong side of the road!" I yelled.

Bento turned around from the passenger seat. He saw my face and laughed. "Hang in there, Sammy. One of the many things you'll get used to. I promise it's the right side over here."

There were cars everywhere, hooting and speeding all over the place and huge roads that crisscrossed over each other, Bento said they were called freeways. I couldn't see much as it was getting dark, but it looked as if there was no open space anywhere, just building after tall building. I must have fallen asleep on the drive and it was almost midnight by the time we arrived at Jeffrey's house. I just remember being shown into the bedroom and climbing into the big cosy bed. I didn't even brush my teeth or change into pajamas. I heard the quiet conversation and laughter from the living room and drifted off to sleep, with the fresh breeze blowing through windows that weren't even covered with burglar bars.

The next few days were a blur. I felt like I was back in kindergarten, learning everything all over again. Jeffrey lived close to a place called Hendry's Beach in Santa Barbara. We walked over there the first day after a breakfast of bagels and cream cheese; never had that before in my life, and they were good. Good Jewish food, Jeffrey had said with a grin. I nearly got myself run over as I crossed the road, looking the wrong way for cars. I had a difficult time understanding the American accent and wondered about all the differences in the same language. Bonnet and boot and petrol didn't seem to exist over here. It was hood and trunk and gas.

The first time I went to the little market down the road, I asked for a cool drink and the lady said, "Well they are all pretty cold, what soda do you want?" Then she laughed at me when I handed over some South African money. I had to figure out how to pay with quarters and nickels and dimes.

We stayed with Jeffrey for about a week.  Maggie and Bento were busy looking for a place to call home and getting things ready for their wedding.  Avo and I hung out together.  I liked him a lot.  He had a kind of craggy face and wore these long shorts and bright shirts with flowers all over them.  He got them in Hawaii, he said.  Nobody in South Africa would wear those for sure.  He never wore shoes, just slip-slops, or flip-flops, as Avo called them.

He took me to visit the zoo and we went hiking up different trails.  Santa Barbara was squished between the mountains and the beach.  Avo, as I had started to call him, always knew some interesting things about animals and plants.  I found out that he had been a professor at the University.  He was quiet but had this kind of twinkle in his bluish-grey eyes and he always looked right at me when he was talking.  He asked me questions about what I thought and how I felt; sometimes I didn't know how to answer him.

We spent most of the time at different beaches.  He knew a lot about the fish and sea life too.  He told me he had just stopped surfing a while ago.  Said he had to slow down a bit now, and thumped his chest.  He showed me his huge boards in the garage.  We spent hours watching the cool surfers at Rincon Point.  That was our favourite beach.  It was a bit of a drive from his house, down the coast to Carpinteria, but we both loved watching the dudes riding the waves there.  I was going to save up my pocket money and get a board for sure.

I was really happy when Bento and Maggie said they had found a place to rent in Carpinteria.  It was up in the foothills, but you could see the ocean.  We moved in there a week before the wedding was going to take place.  It was fun to settle into the house.  I had my own bedroom and even a small room that used to be a closet that I called my study.  We didn't have much furniture, but that didn't seem to matter.

We spent most of the time in the big kitchen that even had a fireplace.  We had a big oak table that was left there; the stove had two ovens and we had an automatic dishwasher, which I had to learn to load.  The only thing I was missing was Rosie.

The day before the wedding, Bento and I had driven the twelve miles from our new home to Santa Barbara to pick up our friends from Nashville.  We had gone to the airport and I was expecting to get them at the terminal, but instead, Bento had driven to another section of the airstrip.  We had watched as this small plane came whizzing in and landed, swoosh, and stopped a short distance away. Out had come Chaz, who was as bald as anything.  His head was like a black bowling ball.  But man, was he big and he looked strong!

"Hi, y'all," he yelled.

A tall dark-skinned lady climbed down the stairs; her long bright pink dress billowing around her and these long rasta braids thumping down her back.

"Lord Amighty, that darn plane seems to get smaller each time we fly in it."  She gave a big stretch.

I laughed.  Sugar was just as I remembered her when she last visited us in Durban a few years before.

"Hey, Morris, you scally-wag, don't you go too far.  Run right to Uncle Bento."  She yelled as a little boy climbed down the stairs from the plane and ran across the tarmac.  He had a mop of dark curls and a pudgy little face that was so black it seemed to glow.

Bento and I walked towards them.  "Wow, imagine just flying in like that!" I said.

"Hey, Sammy.  What's it been?  Three years since we've seen you? You shooting up like a beanstalk."

Chaz came towards us and gave me a big hug.  "Glad we didn't have to fly all the way to Africa to see you this time.  Welcome to the States!  I need some help checking the plane.  You want to give me a hand?"

Bento had scooped up the boy and was twirling him around.  He was giggling like crazy and saying, "Faster, faster, Uncle Beeno."

Chaz and I climbed back into the Cessna.  We examined the instrument panel in the cockpit.  He started to explain some of the dials and I even sat in the pilot seat.  Then we had to check the outside of the plane and sign into the small office for private pilots.

"Dang, how much pocket money would I have to save to get one of these?" I asked Chaz.

"Huh.  This baby will break your piggy bank for sure."  Chaz laughed.

As we walked over to join the others who had unloaded the luggage and were squishing it into the car, Chaz said, "You're going to be hanging out with us for a few days while Maggie and Bento go on their honeymoon.  You want to take a quick spin in Flying Eagle sometime?"

"Hell yes," I blurted out.

He threw an arm around me.  "That's my boy!" he chuckled.

* * *

Morris was kind of cute but did I have to babysit him all afternoon?  He seemed pretty big for five years old and had this funny kind of twang when he spoke.  I guess he had picked it up from Chaz, and living in Nashville.  He followed me around like a puppy dog, which was kind of annoying.  I was trying to help out, as Sugar and Chaz were busy with the wedding stuff.  I remembered him as a chubby little baby when they had visited us in Durban, but I hadn't wanted to be near him that much, it was just too much work. He always seemed to be eating or pooping or crying.  Now at least I could play Legos with him and he liked rocks and sticks and making mud pies.  I even let him carry around Moosey.  I was getting way too old to have that silly stuffed Moose on my bed.

## 12. The Wedding

The wedding was on the beach and then we were going to go back to Jeffrey's for a party. Chaz was going to be Best Man and Sugar was Bridesmaid, I guess it was called. Morris and a little girl, Annie, who lived next door to Jeffrey, were going to scatter flowers. I had laughed and nearly cried and almost wanted to say no when Maggie had asked me to walk her down the aisle. I really didn't want to have everyone look at me and was sure I would trip and goof it all up. But jeez, she didn't have her dad, or anyone else here, that would, so of course, I had to say yes. We were lucky, as we didn't have to get dressed up. The guys wore loose cream-coloured shirts that didn't even tuck in and we wore denims. My first pair of Levi's! And baby Morris had mini-denims on, too. I got my first pair of cool surfer loafers. Sugar and Annie had on flowing dresses that must have been pretty dull for Sugar. They were pale blue, but Sugar had brightened hers up by throwing a turquoise shawl over her shoulders.

We had arrived at the beach and were really happy that the sun was shining and the breeze hadn't picked up. I was surprised to see an archway made of white wicker and decorated with flowers that had been put up on the sand.  There were chairs placed in a semi-circle and a pathway lined with rocks and shells that led up to the arch.  A young guy was sitting to one side, playing guitar.  I was waiting to see the minister who would marry them, when up rocks Avo; his hair tied back in a ponytail and he also wore the same matching shirt and denims.  Avo led me over and positioned me at the last row of chairs, gave me a wink and said I would be fine.

My hands were sweating, even though it wasn't too hot.  It was just right with a few clouds brushing up against the mountains. Jeffrey went and stood in front of the arch and starting talking to Bento, who was looking pretty slick with his hair glossed down and an orchid on his shirt.  Then I realized it was Jeffrey/Avo who was going to marry them.  Things were a little different in California!

We waited a while, but it was fun as people on the beach were gathering around to have a look and the guests started arriving.  Not that many, just some friends of Avo and Bento's and the real estate agent and people that Sugar knew.  It was then I realized that Maggie and I had no family there.  My aunt was getting married and she had no sister, no mom or dad or aunts or uncles or cousins there to celebrate with her.

My heart scrunched up.  My mom and dad were dead.  Granny had been ill and died years ago and Old Papa, who had been in Zim, had died just last year.  Auntie Flo was in a home and couldn't remember anything.  Maggie said that her cousins were scattered all over the world; a few of them were still trying to tough it out in Zim. The rest had thought that moving to a different country would be a better quality of life--Zambia, Australia, New Zealand, England, and Mauritius.

The guests took their seats and the guitar guy turned up the amp so you could hear him above the sound of the ocean, the seagulls swooping past, and the dogs barking at the other end of the beach where they were allowed to run.  Bento and Chaz walked towards the archway and stood to one side.  I could see a car pull up along the road and then Sugar stepped out and Morris and Annie seemed to tumble out.

Sugar grabbed each of them by the hand.  She looked like she was half-scurrying, half-dragging the kids.  I had to smile.  Maggie got out too and her silky cream dress trailed behind her as she made her way down towards us.  As she came closer I could see that she had baby roses threaded through her hair. The dress had a soft neckline with lace peeking out and the sleeves were lacy too. She had on slipslops of rose gold and she held a bunch of roses and orchids.

Morris and Annie had little blue buckets filled with rose petals. Everyone laughed when Morris stopped to pick up some shells and Annie ran back to try to get him. She was whispering to him and trying to show him how to scatter the rose petals. He seemed to get the idea and then really got into it, tossing them up as high as he could with a "wheeee" and a cheeky grin. Sugar followed the kids. She was trying not to laugh, I could tell, and she sort of sauntered down the path, her shawl fluttering in the breeze and her braids, woven with flowers, bouncing as she walked.

Maggie stepped onto the path. She took the bouquet in one hand and I could see her smooth down her skirt. She then cradled the bouquet in both hands and took a breath. She gazed at the guests. She was smiling, but was it my imagination, or were her eyes kind of sad? I wondered if Maggie was thinking of the ones that weren't there too. Maggie walked slowly towards me. She linked arms with me and I smiled nervously.

"Thank you," she whispered as we took the first step along the path.

The guitar guy stood up and started playing another tune and the guests stood up. I tried to walk slowly and stand tall, as Avo had encouraged me to do. I glanced at Bento. He was looking at Maggie as if she was the Mona Lisa or something. We walked forward and stopped in front of Avo. Maggie turned to me and gave me a kiss on the cheek and then Bento stood next to her. I escaped and stood to the side and wiped the sweat from my forehead.

I don't really remember the words of the ceremony. Bento had pulled out the rings from his pocket and there was something about "by the power invested in me by the State of California, I now pronounce you husband and wife." Bento gave Maggie a big smooch and the kids went crazy tossing the petals, and someone else was blowing bubbles, and the guitar guy went crazy with some flamenco style music.

We gathered at Jeffrey's house afterward, some people just walking from the beach and up a few streets, others, including Maggie and Bento took cars. It was a two-story house that had this sprawling garden and a few large trees on the side. There were shutters on the windows that had been painted purple. The bushes in the garden had been trimmed and the flowers scattered to trail along the path. How had I not noticed the beautiful bright bougainvillea and the jacaranda tree that were the same as we had in Africa? The fishpond by the front door had floating candles covering it. The house had been tidied up. All the papers were put away and someone had given it a good cleaning. There were flowers all over the place in Mason jars; roses and lilies and what we called Barberton daisies, from a town in South Africa. There were lots of candles everywhere, in all sorts of candlesticks and glass jars. The guitar guy had brought in some friends, a girl in a long bright skirt and another man with a Mexican hat; he called it a sombrero. They were playing in the living room.

The best part was the food. A lady who lived nearby had been asked to do the cooking. She made all these great dishes: tamales, enchiladas, and spicy rice and beans. There were crispy chips and they had smashed the avocadoes up and called it guacamole or something. I had never had any of it before. I knew I was going to like living in California even more now, because of the Mexican food. The funny thing was, that when I went to see if I could help her put things on the table, I felt as if Rosie from Africa had appeared in another body. At first, I thought she was speaking Portuguese, like Bento, but it was different. She was sort of chunky like Rosie, but her skin was a golden brown and her hair was a lighter colour and straight; not like Rosie's tight black curls. I was patted on the head and she called me hijo, which means son in Spanish. She smiled and hummed a lot. I couldn't believe it when she said her name was Rosita!

Chaz hushed the musicians and clinked his glass till everyone quieted down. "Welcome, y'all. We don't want to interrupt the partying too long, but Jeffrey and I wanted to say a few words on this special occasion. I met our dear Maggie in Africa and am happy to say that because of her, I am the happiest of husbands." He waved to Sugar, who laughed and blew a kiss back to him, "and I am proud to be Dad to young Morris. Thank you, Maggie, for being a special friend and for all you have done for our godson, Sammy." I wasn't expecting that and kind of froze when everyone looked at me. "We wish you and Bento every happiness and expect a visit to Nashville soon."

Everyone laughed. Jeffrey cleared his throat. "I am so grateful that history and the present have merged so beautifully together. Maggie's grandfather and Bento's grandmother knew each other and fate had a way of stepping in, to bring these two, Bento and Maggie, together. Their meeting at Victoria Falls has brought my son back to me. I feared that he would have stayed away in Portugal or kept travelling the world. He has brought me a precious daughter-in-law and grandson."

Jeffrey opened his arms wide as if he was going to hug us then wiped a tear from his eye. "They are my family. California may be a little different from Africa, right Sammy?" He grinned and gave me a thumbs-up sign. "We will do all we can to make this their new home."

The music started again. The crazy Californians were dancing up a storm, with Sugar rocking out with Chaz and young Morris mixed up between them. I escaped to the kitchen again and finished up the guacamole.

Maggie came to find me. She was wearing another pretty dress. My heart skipped a little. It was pale, shiny green and I remembered the feel of the soft silk.

She saw me looking at it. "You remember this, don't you? It was your mom's. It's about the only thing that I have of hers. I wanted to wear it today to have her close to me." She held her hand over her heart. We both stood there for a moment. "We're leaving soon Sammy. Come out while I throw the bouquet."

A group of women had gathered on the area around the fishpond. Maggie stood on the patio and tossed the flowers over her head. There was a lot of laughing and screaming and then the real estate lady shouted, "I got it, I got it!"

I wish someone we knew had caught it. Maggie came over and hugged me. "I know you will have fun here at Jeffrey's with Sugar and Chaz. We will see you in a week, okay?" She held onto me for a long time, so I felt as if I was getting squished to death.

"I am so glad you were here with me Sammy. You made the day so special and I want you to know how happy I am that we are starting this new life together." She pulled away from me and I could see tears in her eyes. "I love you so much."

Boy, she was getting way too sentimental now!

"Have fun," I said. Then it sort of slipped out. "Love you too."

Off they went on their trip to Hawaii and there I was in California, U.S.A., looking forward to learning to surf and taking a trip in Flying Eagle and eating lots more Mexican food.

## 13. Returning
### Free State, South Africa  2000

I could hear my heart beating--thunk, thunk, thunk.  I wiped my hands on my khaki pants and pushed away the damp hair from my forehead.  I was about to go crazy with the pesky mopani flies that were trying to crawl into my eyes.  Damn it was hot--a sultry heat that seemed to seep into the pores of my skin.  The sky was starting to shift colours from a dense, blue bowl that seemed to go on forever, to a few streaks of gold and rose as the sun sank a little lower towards the earth.

"Still Bwana.  No move.  Thula."  Thomas, the African guide beside me, whispered and lightly touched his hand on my shoulder.  "He here, manje."

I could feel my leg tighten up and on the verge of cramping.  We had been crouched in the makeshift lean-to for an hour waiting, waiting.  Through the stacked branches of acacia trees and thatched grass, we could see the endless grassland and scattered, flat-topped thorn trees in front of us.  I licked my cracked lips.  I desperately wanted to take a drink from the water canteen beside me.  I turned my head slightly.  Thomas squatted beside me, so still and so calm.

The heavy Park Ranger uniform must have been suffocating, yet his gaze had not wandered from the bush in front of us.  His breathing was quiet and he didn't stir.

Then, something in his energy changed.  It was as if he sensed the approach of the object of our hunt--as if he was willing them forward to leave the cover of the golden grasses and move across the clearing to the muddy waterhole.

I scrunched up my eyes following his gaze.  I could see nothing but veld.  Just my luck, I thought.  My big African safari and there's not an animal in sight.  We had seen a few springbok on the drive out from the camp.  Their graceful leaping looked like a synchronized dance.  A herd of zebra with their intricate, black and white designer coats, had also crossed our path, but I wanted to see the Big Ones-- lion, leopard, elephant, rhino, and buffalo.  I was striking out.  And I only had a couple of days left.

A slight breeze ruffled the leaves in the tree above us and brought a moment's relief from the cloying heat.  I welcomed in a deep breath. Thomas's body seemed to elongate forward and his hand slowly inched its way down to the rifle that was propped up next to him.  The tall grasses before us shifted and swayed with amber lights dancing in the sun, yet the breeze had stopped.  The movement was so slight that I was sure I was imagining it, but Thomas gave a thumbs-up sign and lifted the gun; every movement as if it was in slow motion.  The grass parted like a golden curtain.  The play was about to begin.

Now my heartbeat quickened, as the head of the most enormous lion emerged into the scene before me.  It was if he was looking straight at us, his eyes glowing and his head framed by the dark halo of mane.  Damn.  I had seen so many photos and movies of the 'King of the Beasts,' but never had I felt such an incredible power and total feeling of awe.  Actually, to tell the truth, it was fear--as Shumba plodded forward, getting ever closer to us.  A second male lion emerged.

"Now," I whispered, "We are totally screwed."

What had possessed me to think this was a good idea?  Yes, I knew Thomas was the head guide and had loads of experience in the bush, but these cats were acting as if they didn't give a darn about the wimpy humans pretending they couldn't be seen or sensed in the pitiful lean-to.  They kept strolling forward, as if out for a Sunday lunch.  And that lunch would most likely be me!  I wondered how long we had.  How long would Thomas wait till he at least attempted to protect us?

He touched the back of my hand.  I had spaced out and now, I felt again, the Nikon camera that was heavy in my palm.  He still wanted me to take a picture?  My boggled brain cleared for a moment and I brought the camera up.  That damn telephoto lens felt as if it weighed a ton.  Now my view of the lions was as clear as could be, every frightening detail.  A part of me was still wondering how they would take us down.  I started to frame my subjects.

I began to sense the direction they would go, where the light would enhance the shot--whir, whir, whir.  I was immersed in the process of getting the best angles and followed them through the lens as they sauntered to the waterhole and began a gentle lap-lap of the muddy water.  Time seemed to hold still on that hot South African evening, and I lost myself in the beauty of the land and the feeling of connection to those immense beasts.  They were in no hurry and after a time, the older lion raised his head and, through the lens, I saw him look right at me.  It was as if our eyes connected.  There was an all-knowing look, an almost condescending look.

I bit my lip.  I felt humble and rather pathetic.  "Thank you," I said.

I felt myself tearing up and the picture blurred.  By the time I had wiped away the moisture from my eyes and lifted the camera to take more shots, all I could see was the flick of a tail as the lions disappeared back into the grassland, and out of view.

"Siyabonga."  Thomas echoed my thanks and laughed.  He gave me a high five.

And that was how, with shaky legs and an incredibly full heart, I made my way to the jeep that bounced on rough, dirt roads back to the safari lodge, to celebrate my twenty-first birthday.

## 14. Reuniting

I wanted to meet on neutral ground, so I had suggested that Peter come to the safari lodge. Maggie and Bento had given me the gift of the safari for my birthday, and although we had all flown over from the States together, they had decided to stay in Durban for the week.

The place was pretty rustic, but that suited me. They were more concerned with the conservation and protection of animals than being a high-end, ritzy tourist trap. I had found out that this had been a working farm and the owners had converted it to a private game reserve when the economy in South Africa started to decline. They had built numerous rondavels, the traditional African huts; round dwellings with thatched roofs. Simple wooden furnishings, handcrafted batik curtains, and bedspreads were in each rondavel. Woven rugs covered the highly polished red concrete floors. There were composting toilets and outdoor showers, screened from observers with thatched awnings, but open to the big African sky.

It was magical taking a shower with the big full moon shining down; Mama Moon who had seemed to guide me since my childhood, sweeping her beam of light through the darkness.

The main lodge had been built using huge poles, thatch, and

recycled materials. Three large rondavels were joined together by wooden, covered walkways. One was the kitchen and dining area, with large wooden tables and benches where meals were eaten community style. The lobby and lounge were the larger areas and the bar and game room formed the third circle.

There had been little contact with Peter over the past ten years; cards and phone calls on special occasions. I had written some letters and sent photos--my first day of high school.

There were no uniforms at this unique school in California. We slept in wooden cabins and spent so much time outdoors, hiking, working in the vegetable gardens, and chopping wood. There had even been dogs and horses on campus. I had been so happy when Maggie had suggested we look at the school. It was about an hour away from where we lived and boarding school had sounded pretty good to me.

I had sent Peter photos of me, Uncle Sammy, with Maggie and Bento's daughter, Sophia, who was now a feisty ten-year-old. There were pictures of me surfing Rincon, my hair pretty long and a lot blonder, and a couple where I was piloting the Flying Eagle, Chaz beside me, of course. Life had been busy. I had gone to the local college in Santa Barbara for two years. Then, deciding that I didn't want to get saddled with outrageous debts, had opted to do what I really wanted--getting my pilot's license.

There had been lots to see and do and I guess I hadn't thought about Peter that much over the years. Maggie had told me that he had been in and out of other treatment centres, but perhaps he had finally gotten the help he needed, as he had been sober for some years now.

When I was eleven, I had walked away from him as he sat at the country club bar the night he had been in a bad accident. My friend Evan had been maimed and his father killed. I had not seen Peter after that final accident and before we flew to America. I had not wanted to see him. I wasn't sure what to expect now and certainly would not have arranged to meet with him if Maggie hadn't insisted.

After all she and Bento had done for me--my private boarding school wasn't cheap and they were helping with the cost of flight training--I felt I needed to do what she asked. I think Maggie wanted to know if Peter was all right. He almost had to spend time in jail because of the accident, but he had been lucky. The autopsy had shown that Boet had actually died of a heart attack and not the impact of the accident, so Peter had not been held accountable for his death.

Evan was another story. He had lost one leg and after countless surgeries and a year in the hospital they had managed to save his other leg, but with limited use. After five years, he was fitted with an artificial limb and learned to walk again. I couldn't believe that Peter would have EVER wanted to have another drink, but I had been to a few Alcoholics Anonymous meetings with Maggie soon after we had settled in California. I learned how drinking was a disease and how even if the person wanted to stop it was very, very difficult. That seemed horribly true.

I had spotted Peter through the large windows as he had entered the lobby and stopped at the reception desk. The lady behind the desk pointed towards the veranda where I was sitting. I swallowed a mouthful of my breakfast, and then pushed the plate away. I wasn't hungry anymore.

As I stood up and pushed back the chair, he came towards me and held out his hand. "Jeez, Sammy. Good to see you. And happy birthday! Can't believe you are twenty-one. Damn, that makes me feel old," he laughed.

I grabbed his hand and gave it a firm shake. I was taller than him by about five inches and I relished looking down on him. No way he was going to push me around again and get away with it.

"Hi, Peter. It was lucky you were driving out this way and could make it. Sorry I didn't have time to come to your place. It's been a busy trip. I'll get the waiter over and get some coffee, shall I?"

"Ja that would be lekker. What's your news? Maggie has a little girl, hey?" Peter asked.

We sat back down and I ordered coffee and a hot chocolate.

I grinned. "Little Sophia is quite a firecracker. Bento says she has too much Portuguese blood running through her. She keeps us all on our toes."

I told him about my schooling and how I was close to getting my charter pilot's license.

"That's good, following what you are interested in," Peter said.

Perhaps he truly had changed. He looked pretty fit. He had lost weight and seemed more relaxed and had even been smiling. I asked him about work. He had a job with an old Zim friend that suited him, as he could work part-time.  He could go to his meetings, which he said were important to him.  Did I know that he had quit drinking?  He also travelled around a bit, doing some sales.  He enjoyed going to different towns and had seen quite a bit of South Africa.

I wanted to ask about my friend, Evan.  Perhaps it wasn't such a good idea to bring it up.  It was weird.  There was a part of me that badly wanted to open up and talk to Peter about things that had happened in the past and how he felt; to have, as Avo always said, a real conversation; a heart to heart.  Here I was at twenty-one, "key of the door" and all that.  There was this knot in my stomach, and the memory of his eyes glaring at me with such loathing and the anger in his voice that made me feel like a kid again.  I wanted to trust him when he said he didn't drink, that he had his shit together, but there was a voice in my head that kept saying, "Don't believe it, Sammy. Don't believe what he says!"

"I wasn't sure what you wanted to do today, but I thought we could go on a game-viewing trip.  They have a tour leaving in a little while.  I can take a guest and it's all included in my package," I said.

It would be way better if Peter and I had something to do instead of trying to make idle conversation all day.

"Sure, that would be good, but I would like to have some time when we get back to catch up a bit more," Peter said as he stood up.

I nodded, wondering what he meant and then I went to sign up for the tour and get a few things from my room.  Thomas was with us, and he greeted me like an old shamwari.  There was also another guide that he was training.

We were just going to be driven around and not walking through the bush as we had a few, should I say, older people with us--a German couple, complete with safari jackets, a couple from Nashville who didn't know Sugar and Chaz, but were fitted out with ten-gallon hats, a lady from Poland, and a bunch of Rotary exchange students from all over.  We piled into the jeep that had been modified for tours.  It had an extra-long body that was open on the sides. Wooden seating had been built and a canvas canopy erected above for protection from the sun.  The students were about my age, some a little younger and very friendly so I was glad to have them.  We soon struck up a conversation and, I'm afraid, I sort of ignored Peter.

I had been away from Africa for ten years.  I had grown to love the States and the people I had met there, but there was something that choked me up as the warm breeze blew across my face. We jostled over the bumpy roads, a cloud of dust billowing behind us. The sun was warm, but the temperature had dropped slightly so it was bearable. I hung on to the side of the jeep and closed my eyes. I could hear the chatter of excitement in the jeep and then the screaming whine of the engine as Thomas shifted gears to go up a steep donga. Layered above those sounds and far off in the distance, I could hear the whaa-whaa cry of a go-away bird and even beyond that, as if in higher and wider circles, the faint, almost dog-like bark of the vultures. If I focused intently, I felt as if I could hear the whispering sounds of the blinkgras being blown about in the wind, and I could imagine the sunlight dancing and reflecting off the silvery, silky tendrils. It was as if I disappeared back into a time and space that I had known as a toddler, growing up on the farm; Africa in my bones, and then beyond that, before birth, the essence of Africa indelibly etched into my soul.

"Hey, Sam. Elephants to the right!" Peter yelled.

I opened my eyes and glanced over to where the students had disobeyed the 'sitting at all-times' rule and were pressed together with cameras clicking away. A herd of elephants in single file started to cross the dirt track in front of us--slow and massive, yet moving with grace and ease. With ears flapping and tails swinging they crossed in front of us undisturbed by the jeep and the ogling tourists in it.

Thomas had stopped the vehicle a fair distance away but had left the engine running and had hushed the passengers as best he could. Both he and the other guide were armed, but I knew enough about the resort now, to know they would only use them in a dire emergency. It was magical seeing the elephants again. I had a hazy memory of big, grey shapes coming into view when Mom, Dad, and I had visited Wankie gamepark those many years ago.

By the time Thomas had done the half-circle of the park, everyone had many photos of zebras, a sable buck with his beautifully curved horns, the long-necked, long-legged, gangly giraffes and, yes, we had a distant viewing of a rhino. Peter had started to chat up the Polish lady who was a writer for a magazine, and I had my eye on a cute girl from Brazil who was impressed with my few sentences of Portuguese and the fact that I had been born in Africa.

## 15. Zimbos to the Rescue

We arrived back at the lodge in time for an early dinner; a braai on the patio. The food looked really good. Lots of salads and freshly baked bread and, of course, I had to instruct the cute Brazilian how to roll the sadza into a ball and dip it into the tomato relish and had to explain what Boerewors was. It had been a while since I had eaten that.

I kept my eye on Peter as we sat there, a part of me on full alert waiting for the tell-tale signs that Peter was enjoying a few cocktails. I expected the loud laugh and the heated conversation to start at any time and felt as if I couldn't quite relax. As I glanced towards him, I couldn't believe it when I noticed the waiter giving him a second Shirley Temple while the other adults helped themselves to the award-winning Cape wines.

At one point, Peter had come over to the younger group. "Sam, we should have a little chat while we can. There's something I need to get off my chest. I'd really like a few minutes with you."

I told him I would just say goodbye to the exchange students who were leaving soon.  It was getting late and they were going to be picked up by the charter bus.  The sky turned from a washed-out pale blue to streaks of copper-red as night fell.  It was then, as if a curtain dropped, the heavy darkness descended.

The screech of tires and brakes caught my attention.  I turned to see what was going on.  The safari lodge Land Rover careened up the rough dirt road, its headlights bouncing up and down.  It came to a rapid stop in the parking lot.  The two guards in their khaki uniforms came flying out of the vehicle and ran towards the lobby.  I could hear a flurry of conversation in English and what I thought might be Zulu.  Most of the guests seemed oblivious, but the waiters who had served our dinner looked concerned and muttered to each other.  I glanced at Peter and, he too had picked up on the drama.  He gave me a nod and walked off to the lobby.  I said my goodbyes to my new friends quickly with promises of keeping in touch with some of the cute gals.  Then I went to see what was happening.  Gerry, the owner of the lodge who was an ex-Zimbabwean, was at the lobby desk in a conversation with the guards and Peter.

As I came forward he reached for the phone.  "They have found some animals down.  Poachers," Peter said grimly.  Gerry is trying to get some help, but we are going to go out and see if we can track the skelms."

"You are going?" I asked, a little confused.

"Ja, I said I'd like to give a hand.  Gerry and I were actually in the same R.L.I. unit."

I had forgotten that Peter had lived through the Rhodesian Bush War.  He had shown me some pictures once and had told me about his service in the Rhodesian Light Infantry.  Every Rhodesian male had been on call up as soon as they left school.

"The national park guys are miles away at Kruger Park, and they are always a bit reluctant to send their men onto a private reserve.  Gerry has four guys that he has trained.  We will take a scout around.  The bastards are probably long gone by now!" Peter exclaimed.

"Don't you think you should hold off till you get some other help?  I know the poachers nowadays are armed and pretty ruthless.  It's been a few years since you guys were in the army," I said with a bit of a smile.

"Hey, we can't just let them high-tail it out of here.  We'll be fine.  Sam, you had better stay here," he said in a serious voice.

I noticed the light of excitement in his eyes. "I don't want to be responsible for anything happening to you. We will check in at the lobby with the ham radios. You can reach us if you need. Sorry this had to happen, but I'm glad I can be of some use."

The guards and Gerry were coming out of the back office with rifles and a couple of Uzis and F.N's. I gasped as I recognized them. Gerry handed one to Peter who took it without hesitating, his hand cradling it with a familiar grip. He had not forgotten how to use it. There was more coming and going; backpacks loaded and ham radios checked. Peter had gone to his car and brought out a well-worn army jacket. He changed into long hiking pants and sturdy boots. Within a short time, the men were ready.

Before he left, Peter turned towards me. "I'm chuffed I got to see you. I'm proud of what you have done." He paused. He seemed to struggle with the words. "I'm sorry I wasn't always there for you in the way that I should have been." He put the gun down carefully by his backpack and as he stood up, I thought I glimpsed tears in his eyes. "Right then, I guess that will have to do. Wish we had a bit more time. You are supposed to leave the lodge tomorrow right? I'm not sure when we will be back. Cheers then, my boy. You take care, all right? You're doing really well. It seems America suits you," he said with a soft smile.

I regretted that I hadn't taken more time to be with him. We had had a good day. My mind went back to my tenth birthday. He had given me my first camera and we'd had a good day then, too, at the beginning. Perhaps we had both grown and changed. Perhaps we would be able to be more in contact now; heal the past and "support each other"--another of Avo's favourite sayings. I hoped so. I knew my mom, wherever she was floating about in the heavens, would have wanted that. I realized now, that she and Peter had shared something special.

We shook hands. He was standing with his back towards the large window, his body framed by the glow of the moon that was rising into the night sky. As I looked at him, I had this weird feeling, as if I was looking at an older version of myself. How had I never noticed that Peter had this sort of cowlick as well? I guess his hair was longer now. His eyes peered into mine, with an intensity that startled me. Were they the same colour green as mine, or was that a trick of the moonlight too?

He was still grasping my hand and then he pulled me into a hug and held on for a long time. A part of me wanted to push away. I was getting embarrassed. He let me go and then turned, picked up the backpack and gun and walked away. I watched him as he went from the lobby to the Land Rover. The other men piled in. He sat for a moment and then his head turned towards me and he caught my eye. He waved goodbye. I watched as they drove away.

It had taken me a while to go to sleep. I had thought that I would check with the lobby during the night to see if there had been any news, but I woke up with the bright African sun shining through the crack in the curtain. I dressed quickly and hurried to the lobby. The night receptionist was just going off duty. She had heard from Gerry twice during the night. They had found the trail of the poachers near the border of the reserve and were going to try to track them before they made their way across the boundary. They had not found any animals as yet. I was restless and frustrated that I wasn't doing anything to help.

The morning passed slowly. The majority of guests had left and they had cancelled the morning sightseeing tour, as a safety measure. By midday, two National Park trucks from Kruger had arrived. They were in contact with Gerry and were going to go out and rendezvous with them.

My connection to the States came in very useful. The head Ranger, Hennie, had a sister that had moved to California and I promised that I would take a few things from South Africa back for her. I managed to talk my way into going with them, to link up with Gerry and his crew. As I didn't have my own equipment, they supplied me with a canvas backpack with dry rations, water bottle, torch, and numerous other items. It was when Hennie asked if I had any experience with firearms, that I smiled. I had never told Maggie or Peter, but I had handled both an Uzi and F.N. before. Good old Chaz had been my instructor when he came to California on some work-related business.

We had spent a week camping out on a friend's farm not far from where I had gone to high school. I was nineteen when he told me stories of his time flying to the Nata Reserve and meeting me as a young boy. He taught me so much that week. I had done a lot of camping and hiking, but he showed me skills about surviving in the bush--making a fire without matches, tracking, feeding myself from the land, emergency first aid, and the tricks and techniques he had learned as a Green Beret. He insisted that I learn how to use a pistol and an automatic weapon. His buddy had quite a collection. Chaz said I needed to know how to take care of myself in this crazy world. Some pretty gnarly self-defence tactics were also thrown in. We forged a strong bond and I grew up a lot in those few days.

It was early evening when the Kruger Park patrol and I contacted Gerry on the ham radio to say we were close to the border of the park and to find out their location. We ditched the trucks and had been walking for about an hour through the dense bush. Gerry had replied, saying they had the poachers on the run and were quickly catching up to them. They had them visually on several occasions and he thought it was a small group and they would be able to 'deal with them.'

After another half an hour, Hennie tried to reach them again, without success. Dusk was falling when we heard the gunshots. They were amplified in the open veld with no other sounds but our boots tromping on the dry grass and the call of birds. We quickened our pace. It wasn't long before the light began to fade. We heard the solemn hooting of an owl. It seemed to echo foreboding. A large shape blocked the path in front of us. The men brought out two large torches and shined the beams in front. My stomach contracted and a wave of nausea washed over me. A large eland buck lay on its side, bloody and broken. The horns had been hacked from the beautiful head. The skull was smashed and one eye lay suspended and staring upward towards the heavens. We could hear shouting up ahead and another volley of gunfire.

As we continued forward and pushed aside the tall grass, we saw Gerry sprawled on the ground, clutching his arm, while a guide and Peter knelt beside him. "Thank God you guys are here," Gerry said. "I've just got a bullet graze. I'll be okay. The other guards have gone after them. Hurry before it's completely dark."

Peter turned to look as we came forward. He frowned. "What the hell you doing here Sam? I thought I told you to stay put! This is not a picnic we are on. And what are you doing with that damn Uzi? Do you even know how to fire the bloody thing?"

"Looks like you could use some help here and yes, I do know how to handle it. Do you think Chaz would have let me grow up without knowing how to take care of myself?" I retorted. "Let me take a look at that wound. I know how to do that too."

I went over to Gerry to check his arm. "Someone better get going soon," Gerry said.

Hennie and the guards headed off at a sprint. Peter stood up. "Okay, if you think you can handle it." He gave me a penetrating look and turned and ran after Hennie.

I found some supplies in the well-prepared backpack, dressed the wound hastily, and dosed him with some painkillers. "Okay for now?" I asked. "We will have to get that looked at when we get back to the lyepodge."

I settled him against a tree trunk, gave a thumbs-up to the guide that stayed with him and then picked up the Uzi and ran to catch up to the rest of the search party. I couldn't hear anything, but I could see the direction that they had gone; the long grass being trampled and pushed aside.

After a few minutes, I saw something ahead. Catching a glimpse of somebody in the distance, I quickened my pace, thankful that I had developed a practice of daily running. As I drew closer, the person slowed down and then stopped. It was Peter. He bent forward, swaying a little as he did so.

I closed the gap and could hear his rapid breathing as I came up to him. "Peter, you okay?"

His back was towards me. The grip on his gun loosened and it slipped from his hand, falling onto the hard earth. His knees started to buckle. I rushed forward to face him. I expected to see a wound; a bullet hole; blood, but there was nothing. His face was pale and contorted on one side. Slowly he sank lower and lower. I reached out to steady him, but I was unprepared for the weight of his body and we tumbled to the ground. I pushed myself up and knelt over the still form. His eyes were closed. I swallowed. I could feel my heart beating rapidly. Peter's head lolled to the side and a trickle of drool ran from his lips. I placed my fingers on his neck and held my breath. I waited. I couldn't feel anything. No pulse. I moved my fingers slightly, and then I felt the faint beat under them. My breath released in a sigh.

Struggling to pick him up, I cursed as I tried to cradle his body and hold onto the weapons. I couldn't leave them. The short distance back to Gerry felt as if it took forever. A mixture of fear, anger, and frustration washed through me.

The guide saw me and ran to help as I came closer. "Jeez. What happened?" Gerry exclaimed.

"He just collapsed. Must be a stroke or heart. We are going to have to let Hennie and his boys deal with the poachers. We have to get back as soon as we can," I insisted.

"Right. I'll radio the lodge now and get them to bring the Land Rover and contact the Flying Medic service. We will have to walk until we get to the boundary road." Even in his wounded state, Gerry took charge. He was able to contact Hennie to let him know what had happened.

It was a strange procession moving through the now dark night. The guide and I took turns carrying Peter. Gerry held the powerful torch to light the way, but still, we stumbled over anthills and dongas. The unnerving sound of hyenas pierced the night. I remembered the dreadful yip-yip of the impisi from my childhood. It was enough to make your blood run cold.

It seemed as if that walk would never end. Our arms were aching and our clothing was torn from bushes by the time we saw the welcome headlights of the Land Rover. We bounced over the rough, dirt road. There was nothing else out there but the dense, heavy dark. I cradled Peter's head in my lap, and I was aware of every slow breath that entered his body.

We made a quick stop at the lodge where I gathered my things from my rondavel and packed as quickly as I could. I telephoned Maggie and left a message saying we were flying to the hospital in Durban. I had to go with him. It was after ten when we met the plane on the dirt runway. The emergency crew made Peter as comfortable as possible, while the pilot readied for take-off. I was not in the cockpit this time. I sat watching the flurry of activity around the still form of this man that I had known since childhood; this man that I didn't know if I loved or hated.

## 16. Unexpected News

My whole world--my life until this point--felt as if it had been turned upside down.  One of Chaz's aerobatic tricks in Flying Eagle was nothing compared to what I experienced when Maggie told me the news.

An ambulance had met the plane in Durban and once at the hospital, Peter had been taken into intensive care.  It was after midnight.  I had left word with Maggie and expected to see her in the morning.  I was surprised when I saw her rushing through the waiting room door.

"Oh God Sammy, I'm so sorry you had to go through this.  Have you heard any news yet?"  A frown creased her brow.  She ran a hand through her hair, cut short, with a few silver-grey streaks surrounding her face.  She came over and gave me a hug.  "Tell me what happened.  It sounded pretty bizarre.  Something about poachers and tracking them down and Peter collapsing."

I filled her in on the night's activity and then we sat waiting.  There was only one other young couple seated at the far end of the room.  They held each other closely and looked as if they had fallen into an exhausted sleep.  It wasn't long before a doctor came through the swinging doors.  He asked if we were relatives.  Maggie hesitated and then said she was an old friend. We were told that Peter had suffered a stroke. He was breathing on his own but it was unclear at present if he had suffered brain damage, or what use of his limbs he would have. There would be more tests tomorrow. There was nothing else that could be done and he suggested we get some rest.

I went with Maggie back to her hotel that was a short distance away. Bento and Sophia were asleep. We crept in and I settled onto the pull out couch in the mini living room. I was exhausted and collapsed into a deep sleep.

It was after nine o'clock when I woke up. It was quiet and I made a cup of coffee and went to shower. I heard Maggie's voice on the phone. She was just completing the call as I went back into the living room. She slowly put the telephone receiver down and stood still. It looked as if she were about to cry.

"Bento has taken Sophia to an art show," she said turning towards me. "Sammy, I need to tell you something."

"What's happened to Peter?" I asked.

"He is in much the same condition. They will be doing more tests now." She slumped into the chair and was silent for a while. Then she looked up at me. "This is something that I should have told you a long, long time ago." She bent her head and sobbed.

I walked over to her and put my hand on her shoulder. "What is it, Maggie?"

"Oh God, Sammy, I don't know where to start." She lifted her head and a smudge of tears lined her face. "I'm so sorry. I was just trying to take care of you and it never seemed the right time. I wanted to, but with all the drama and the way that he acted I just thought it would be best to let things…." She stood up and started pacing back and forth then sat down again.

"You talking about Peter?" I sank into the chair across from her.

She had taken a breath and wiped away her tears. "I couldn't believe it myself at first." Her voice rose in volume. "I never knew why your mom would not have told me. She didn't even share this with her own sister." She shook her head. "And then each year it seemed harder and harder to…."

"Maggie!" I knew my voice was harsh. "I don't know what you are trying to tell me."

She looked at me and her eyes were filled with pain. There was a long pause. I was just about to speak when she stood up again and walked towards the window. She stopped and looked outside, then turned around.

She spoke quickly and I had to lean forward to catch her words. "James was not your dad. He raised you from the day you were born, but he was not your father."

I shook my head, trying to take in what she was saying. "What do you mean? Not my dad?"

She walked towards me and stood looking down at me. Her voice was brittle as she said, "I only found out after your mom and James had died. When I came from Canada to get you. You were six then. Shelly left a letter. Peter found it when he went to the farm and got some of your things after the raid." Her voice cracked. "The letter was for Peter, telling him about you."

"Why would she leave a letter for Peter?" I gulped. A flash of recognition had me gasp out loud, "Oh God no." My head started to throb. "Are you telling me that Peter is my father?"

Her tears had stopped and Maggie just nodded. I turned and walked quickly towards the kitchenette. I grabbed the cup of now cold coffee, downed it and then thumped the cup onto the table. It broke into pieces. I walked over to the window. I could see the small park down the road. A few kids were playing on the swings. A man was pushing a young boy and together they smiled, enjoying the beautiful sunny day. It felt as if a knife was penetrating my heart.

"Papa," I said in a choked voice. I remembered James swinging me on the old tyre swing under a huge flamboyant tree; the sweet times with James as we explored the farm. The special things he had done for Mom and I. The way he would always tuck me into bed and pat me on the head with a, "slaap lekker, my kind." He was a quiet man, but I had always felt his deep, solid presence. I always felt safe with him.

Now my world was shattered.

I turned around and spitting out the words at Maggie said, "You mean that bastard that tried to beat the shit out of me and left me to fend for myself and forgot about feeding me and could have killed me if I had been in the car when he crashed it--he's my father? You have left it for so long. Why are you telling me now?"

"I'm sorry, Sammy. Please...I think...." She hesitated again. "Peter may not recover. I thought you had to know."

"And if this hadn't happened, would you have ever told me? Nice birthday present, Maggie." My voice was rough as I said, "I'm twenty-one and finally find out that my dad is a raging alcoholic, who is probably dying as we speak." My hand instinctively ran through my hair. I yelled, "I've got to get out of here!" and walked towards the door.

"Sammy, please!" Maggie stood up and walked towards me. "I know this must be an awful shock. Please let's...."

I left the hotel, leaving the shards of my coffee cup on the table without saying another word to Maggie.

## 17. The Visit

I walked the six blocks to the beach, but it was so busy as the Sunday crowd of sun worshipers had gathered. I kept on walking, my head spinning with thoughts bombarding me. Maggie had done all she could for me and I know her life had been crazy too. She had lost her mom, then her sister and her dad. She had lost her country. She had taken care of me and given me all she could, but I always had this feeling that something about my past, something about my life, didn't add up. There had been so many questions that I never thought to ask. Why had Mom kept the family name of Morris? Why had she stayed on the dangerous Nata Reserve? Why had Maggie and I moved to South Africa? Why had I always had this place deep inside that felt so out of kilter?

I guess there are times when you look back on your life and recognize that the gut knowing was always there, but the voice so faint that you didn't listen, or didn't want to listen. There were moments, especially when I grew older, that an incident, or something that was said, would spark a fleeting question in my mind, but I would brush it aside. My mom was dead. I had thought my father was dead too.

After half an hour I found myself wandering through the neighbourhood where Maggie and I had lived with Bento. I walked towards the house and it looked pretty much the same. I stood at the gate, uncertain what to do next, when a figure appeared, walking away from the house towards me. It couldn't be!

I found my eyes tearing up, as Rosie came forward. She had stayed on working for the people who rented the house. She was hunched over and walked with a slow shuffle. She did not see me until she opened the gate and looked up. Her face was lined with wrinkles and she was much thinner than I remembered. Her well-worn dress hung loosely around her. I noticed the curls peeking from under her doek were now white. She was frowning and she hesitated to lift the gate latch.

"Rosie?"

"Yes, Baas?"

"Rosie. It's me. It's Sammy." I smiled at her.

"Sammy?" She gazed at me intently.

Damn. She still hadn't gotten glasses. She shook her head in disbelief.

"It's Sam–Sam," I said.

"Ikona!" She clapped her hands in the traditional African greeting and smiled. "Ah, Maiwee. Sam–Sam."

She came through the gate and stood, looking up at me. She grabbed me around the waist and gave me a hug. She told me that she had kept working so that she could send money back to her family in Zimbabwe. She still lived in the same place, even though South Africa was now a free country. It didn't seem to have helped her very much. She had been given the day off, as she had stayed that Saturday night to look after the two children. She was just leaving to go home.

"I want to go with you," I blurted out.

She gave me a perplexed look.

"I have nothing to do today. Let me come back with you."

"Ah, Sam–Sam. That's not so good I think. She shook her head. Why you here in South Africa?"

"I'll tell you on the bus. Come on. I know you will miss it if we wait." I started walking towards the bus stop. I needed to go with her, perhaps because she had been the one thing I could count on when I was staying with Peter. She had been the closest person I had to family.

I knew that things had changed in South Africa since apartheid had been abolished, but honestly it didn't feel like it was any different. I rode on the dilapidated bus with Rosie. I was the only white. Others looked me at with curiosity and some with hostility. I could tell Rosie felt uncomfortable. We drove past the areas I was familiar with and then headed further out of town. The roads were in worse condition and the buildings looked in need of major repairs. Homeless people sat on the sidewalks and the African children I saw were scantily dressed and, as I remembered from the farm, most were without shoes. The mini-buses were laden with people and the drivers seemed intent on speeding as fast as they could, dodging the bicycles, pedestrians, and African women with huge bunches of bananas balanced on their heads.

I told Rosie about my birthday and that Maggie, Bento, and their daughter were in Durban too. She smiled at that.

We arrived at the cinderblock-housing complex where she lived. It was not called an African Township now; Africans were able to live in different areas, but life for most of them was just as hard and little had changed in the quality of their lives. From the bus stop, we walked down a narrow dirt road. A row of tin-roofed, concrete dwellings lined each side of the road. There were small yards in front, a few with a patch of mealies growing or a trail of flowering pumpkin blossoms, but no lawns or flowers grew in this neighbourhood.

Hesitantly, Rosie led me towards her home. I wondered if I had done the right thing in coming to view her life. Had I put her on the spot? She led me through a wooden gate towards the iron door.

Rosie had two small bedrooms. The concrete floors had a couple of woven rugs and I smiled as I recognized the patterned curtains on her small bedroom window and the side table by her twin bed. Maggie had given them to her when we left.

The second bedroom had two beds and one wooden table. She had a couple of young men come in to sleep there to help pay the rent. They were gone most of the time, working their two jobs. There was an area for preparing food--a propane stove, a mini-fridge, and a wooden counter could hardly be called a kitchen. The only running water was outside at a large sink. The toilet was outside as well. She had a small area in front of the house that she had swept clean. Two old wooden chairs had been placed there, I recognized them as well, and she invited me to sit.

She made a cup of tea and handed me the tin mug. I sipped the very sweet, milky tea and closed my eyes. It tasted delicious and seemed to nurture my soul. The people walking by were obviously surprised to see a young white man visiting. I told Rosie about my life in America and, as I was speaking, I realized how comfortable, affluent, and incredibly easy it must sound to her. My white skin had given me a ticket to paradise. I told her about Peter.

She looked sad. "Ah, Baas Peter. He has the bad spirits with him. The bad Shumba spirits. You be careful now, Sam-Sam. You be careful those same bad spirits don't shuppa you. Okay?"

I laughed. "Don't you worry, Rosie. One Shumba beer and I get drunk."

I had not gotten into the drinking and party phase at college, thank goodness. I sat for a while, silent. Jeez, had I instinctively known that I would have to watch the alcoholic tendency that ran in families; that my bloodline might carry those genes?

Rosie asked if I was hungry and I realized I'd only had a little to eat for almost two days. She seemed pleased to have something to do and went into her house while I sat listening to the tinny radio playing next door--some funky music that sounded like a cross between African hip-hop and reggae. There was laughter from the children down the dirt street. A few dogs barked.

A procession of people walked by dressed in what must have been their best clothes. The women had doeks or hats on their heads and the men wore long trousers and long-sleeved shirts, some with ties. A man dressed in a black shirt and trousers with a white clerical collar around his neck was leading them. He stopped when he saw me. He was tall and lean. His short dark curls had a hint of grey around the forehead.

He took off his hat and said, "Good morning."

He waved the people on and they slowly walked by, obviously curious. He stepped towards the gate and I stood up and went towards him.

"You visiting our sister? We missed her in church this morning. Is she alright?"

"Rosie? Yes, she is fine. She is making me some food. Shall I call her?"

"No, no." He paused. "But I must say, I am interested. I haven't seen you visiting us before. I am Reverend Mkwanazi." He smiled and held out his hand.

I reached out and shook it and it came as a shock to me that I had never greeted an African in this way. Well, of course, I had spent loads of time with Chaz and Sugar. Why did it seem that the colour of their skin didn't matter to me? Was it just the people in Africa that I had shunned? Well, that wasn't true with all of them. Rosie and that young rascal Morris, who had just turned fifteen, had been given plenty of my attention and hugs.

I think I might have blushed, as I felt my face grow warm. "Oh, I am Sam. Rosie used to work for us a long time ago before we moved to America. I'm just here on holiday and saw her at the house we used to live in."

"Ahhhh." He nodded. "Yes. You must have been a lot smaller then, hey?" He lifted his hand high as if he was measuring me and chuckled. "I remember her telling me about you, Sam-Sam."

I couldn't believe he would remember the name Rosie used to call me. He chuckled again at my surprised expression.

"I have a very good memory." He pointed at his head. "May I ask how you like living in America?"

I motioned to the chair and asked him to sit. We fell into an easy conversation. He was soft-spoken, but I could sense strength and calmness in him. Rosie had come out with a plate of sadza and some cooked greens. I wasn't sure what they were, but I was hungry. She greeted her pastor and went back inside and gave him a plate, which, I'm sure, was her lunch. I don't know why, but she said she had to visit a friend for a few minutes and left the two of us together. With simple questioning the discerning man had me tell of my life in Zimbabwe. I told him, between bites of the bland food, of the farm, my mom, and James. I told him how they had been murdered. How my aunt had come back from Canada to take care of me.

"I know of your family, Sam," he said looking at me with his dark, penetrating eyes. "I too, like many others here, have come from Zimbabwe. I too, like Rosie, lived in Matabeleland close to the Nata Reserve. I knew of Madam Morris and how she spent time at the Methodist mission where she had family ties. I am sorry for the loss of her and her husband. Yes. Deeply sorry."

We finished eating. He took my empty plate and he carefully

placed both of them beside him on the floor. "I am also in the Methodist church. I was lucky and they helped me get a transfer to South Africa. I needed to get out of Zimbabwe rather quickly, I'm afraid." He gave no reason why.

He leaned forward in his chair. "I am honoured to meet a relative of the great Reverend Simon Morris, your great-grandfather. I was not able to visit his school, Ingwezi, but we heard a great deal about all the wonderful things that were accomplished, and even today it is amazing that it is still surviving."

Sitting there in a rickety wooden chair, my belly not quite filled from the simple meal, I was at peace. I felt as if the strong lineage from my ancestors and the powerful, resilient energy of the place where I was born was washing through me. I felt a settling of those churned up emotions that I had experienced, not only in the last few days but also as far back as I could remember. This man, who I had never met before, felt like an old, old friend. I smiled as I thought of how he and Avo would have bonded instantly. I wished that they could have met.

We sat in silence. The soft coo-cooing of a mourning dove in the mulberry tree across the road soothed me. Africa and the sound of the doves would forever be intertwined in my heart.

"Reverend, can I share something with you? Something that just happened today?" The words slipped out without me thinking.

He nodded slowly. "Of course, Sam-Sam. We Zimbabweans have to stick together right?"

He sat and held my gaze as I shared the news I had received. I must have spoken for a long time, telling him about my past, but his attention never wavered, and at one point he reached over and patted my leg.

The tears slipped down my cheeks. "I don't know how to change the way I feel. I don't know how to forgive him. I don't know how to forgive Maggie." I stopped talking. He didn't say anything for several minutes.

"I wonder," he said at last, "what your great-grandfather would have done? I heard, a very long time ago from my grandfather, that Simon Morris was also faced with a similar situation. They had many hardships founding the mission and school. It was way back in the 1900s. There were many Africans that stood in the way. At one point, I am told, there was a fire in the church and even a bizarre incident where all the people in the compound were given a powerful muti, which killed a couple of them. After that, there was an epidemic, flu I think it was. The Reverend had a choice to assist the culprits. One man, in particular, would have died if Reverend Morris had not helped him." He smiled his sweet smile again. "I'm sure that counts as forgiveness."

I could see Rosie walking slowly back up the road towards us. She looked so old.

My new friend stood up and touched my head lightly with a well-worn hand. "This is all a shock for you right now, so don't try to force forgiveness to come out. Hambe gashle. In time, you will know from your heart what is right. I am glad you came to share God's day with us."

He slowly turned and walked away, saying farewell to Rosie as he departed.

I knew Maggie must be frantic. We were supposed to catch our flight back to the States tomorrow. I had no idea what condition Peter was in today.

Rosie hugged me and I slipped the few rand that I had in my pocket into her hand. I wondered if I would ever see her again. I promised myself that I would make sure to send her some money every month.

I made my way to the bus stop and waited in the long line. That feeling of straddling different worlds was still present, as much as I tried to believe I could bridge it. Could I resolve having a family I hadn't known about, while still mourning the loss of those I loved? The difference between the colour of my skin and those around me? The gap of living on two different continents? I was born in Africa. I was an African, and still the only white face on the bus.

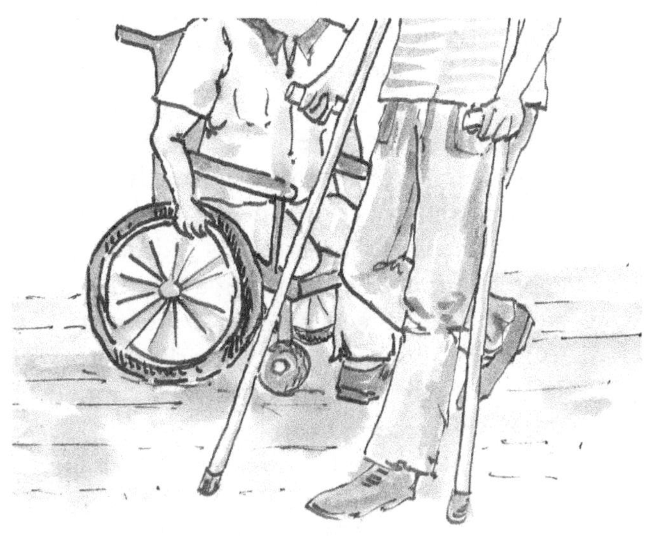

## 18. A Hero

I delayed my flight back to the States for three days. I wanted to visit Peter again before I left Africa. Maggie, Bento, and Sophia needed to get back, and I said goodbye to them at the hotel the next morning.

Maggie and I hadn't had an opportunity to talk yet, so I spoke quietly to her while Bento and Sophia were loading the suitcases into the shuttle bus. "I'm sorry Maggie. It couldn't have been easy for you taking me on and dealing with Peter and knowing the truth. It's something that I will have to try to adjust to and deal with."

She gave me a hug. I took a deep breath and my voice came out rough. "I just want to say thank you for all you have done."

She didn't say anything else but gave me another squeeze and as she walked out of the door she blew me a kiss.

I went back to the hospital after they left. Peter was still in a coma, but the tests seemed to indicate no extensive brain damage. It would be a matter of waiting to see what occurred.

I was making my way to the cafeteria mid-afternoon when I passed a group of young people entering a room on the other side of the hallway. I waited for them, as many of them were on crutches, some in wheelchairs. All seemed to be amputees--legs or arms missing. I stepped forward and held open the door to allow them to enter.  I glanced inside.  There were chairs placed facing the front of the room, and spaces where those in wheelchairs had started to manoeuvre themselves.  At the front of the room sat a young man. He was chatting to a couple of boys that were on crutches.  He looked towards the door and I froze.  We stared at each other for a moment and then a huge smile spread across his face.  He came towards me--his loping walk was slow and unsteady, joggling between right and left legs.  His dressy black trousers hid his legs, and I could tell that under his polo shirt he had a strong upper body.

"I don't believe it!"  He came closer and stood in front of me.  He reached out a hand and I grasped it, thinking that perhaps he needed to be steadied.  The red hair, and the eyes now framed by designer glasses, reminded me of someone from years back.

"Sammy, it's so good to see you.  What are you doing here?"  The voice was deeper but had the same accent I had known years ago.

"Evan?"  I stood stunned.  He looked so different.  He was tall and I could even say good looking.  His whole demeanour was confident and happy.  I told him briefly about Peter.

He shook his head. "I'm so sorry to hear that.  I had hoped that things would have turned the corner for him."  He paused.  "I blamed him for a long time."  He adjusted his stance and I could tell that one leg seemed shorter than the other.  "I just have a few minutes as my little talk starts soon. Perhaps we can meet afterwards. I try to give these kids a bit of encouragement and positive energy." He looked down towards his legs. "You know Sammy, looking back, that accident gave me my life.  It was a long, hard road but now I have something to dedicate myself to.  I travel around the country and try to inspire those that have been injured to keep their faith and know they can be an important contribution to society."  He paused. "I give lectures at treatment centres and support groups too."

We shook hands again and I watched him take centre stage and thank the audience as they started to clap.  He was obviously well known.  I felt tears welling up as I listened to him tell the story of his accident--the battle to live, and then to learn to walk again, with one leg amputated just below the hip and the other below the knee.  He spoke of resilience, of forgiveness, of trust.

I stepped out of the room and quietly closed the door, wishing that I could embrace his compassion and peace.  I wasn't able to do that yet.  I left Africa with no words spoken between Peter and I.  He lay in a coma, and I had not been able to acknowledge to those at the hospital, or to that still form in the bed, that he was my father.

## 19. Brothers Unite
## Los Angeles, California  2006

I had arrived just before dawn.  I was exhausted and the usual problem of finding a parking space near Mo's apartment in Culver City frustrated me.  Hauling a couple of bags from my Jeep, I made my way to the second floor of a sparse apartment complex.  A sad-looking fern in a large clay pot stood to one side of his door.  I searched for the key that was always hidden there and then turned empty-handed to the bright blue door and knocked.  I knew the doorbell didn't work.  I waited for a minute and then knocked again.

"Mo.  Let me in."  I tried to keep my voice as low as possible.

He had a grouchy old man living next door.  "Morris!"  I thumped on the door again and heard some movement behind it.  The lock turned.

"What the hell, Sam!"

The man, who stood before me naked except for a towel wrapped around his waist, was an imposing sight.  He looked older than his 21 years.  If I had met him on a dark night, in a dark alley, I would have, as they say, been scared shitless.  His large head was covered with a mass of dark curls.  His skin was a luminous rich black.  He had a firm jaw and he sure did turn heads and he knew it; and enjoyed it!

"Hey, I did call. Sorry. Where is the damn key?" I muttered.

"You okay, shamwari? What's going on?" Mo asked, opening the door to let me in.

"Bloody awful fight with Tanya. She told me to get out." I dumped my bags on the floor.

"Hey, no sweat. Jeez, that didn't last long. How many girls you gone through now?" He turned his head towards the bedroom door. "You know, I'm a little tied up right now."

I shook my head and grinned. "You think that surprises me? Go back to bed. I know where the couch is. Just try to keep it down okay? And try to get the right name this time, if you introduce her."

Mo slapped me on the back and disappeared into the room as a faint voice called out, "Morris? Where are you, baby?"

I chugged down a glass of water in the minute kitchen and lay on the couch. I couldn't sleep. I was pretty sure that this was it for Tanya and me; both of us had said things we shouldn't have and it would be hard to repair the damage. I found an old sleeping bag in the corner of the couch and bundled up and finally drifted into a restless sleep.

I heard the whistle of the kettle and the aroma of coffee from the kitchen. I sat up and yawned. A once-white wicker rocking chair, a rough handmade coffee table, and a pile of bright cushions filled the space. There were a few posters on the wall and a long, dangerous looking spear stood in one corner.

Mo sauntered through. He had on a pair of loose patterned pants and a sweatshirt. He handed me a mug of coffee and perched on the edge of the rocking chair, his huge body blocking the view to the small window that filtered in the morning light.

"Well, Sam–Sam, fill me in."

I turned my head towards his bedroom and asked, "We in the clear?"

"Yup, I had to get her out before she saw you and got taken in by that cute white boy act. I actually like this one a lot, so not letting you near her for a while; till I get her hooked!"

"You don't have to worry about me. I think I'm going to be laying low for a while. Had a doozy of a fight with Tanya. I can't seem to get this relationship thing right. Way too much drama for me!" I took a gulp of coffee and scrunched my face. "God Mo, this tastes awful. Is this that instant crap?"

"Now, my friend, I don't believe that." Mo laughed, ignoring my previous comment. "I give you a couple of weeks at the most before you have someone after that African hide of yours."

"Huh. You can talk. You have the full packet. Nice shiny black mug and rugby butt. Too bad about the southern drawl." The twang was still so unexpected. Nashville had been his home. "Nobody seems to believe I'm an African with my pale skin and my accent is always thought to be English, Australian or Kiwi. I don't think anyone has ever guessed it right." I yawned again.

"Well, we are just a pair of misplaced Zimbos. At least you don't have to explain that you were found abandoned in a box on a Methodist Mission." Morris chuckled. With his 6-foot, 3-inch frame and broad shoulders, it was hard to believe he could have squished into a cardboard box!

I laughed. Morris caused a stir wherever he went; which was both good and on some occasions, had been pretty bad. I had known him practically all my life. Many times I had been very, very thankful that I called him friend and brother, and had him on my side.

"Hey, I better check what's going on with work. I took a couple of days off to have this relaxing time with Tanya. May as well see if there are any gigs lined up that I could take on now. What are you up to today?" I asked.

"Well, I've already done my run and worked out while you were passed out there. You want to come with me to the studio? I've got a meeting with some new producer that Charlie set me up with. You can sit in and perhaps you can get a two-bit acting part as well. Hey, how did you like that ad I did in my cute polka dot boxers? Drive down Wilshire Boulevard and you can see me showing off that rugby butt!" He turned his back towards me and thrust out his bottom, giving a big laugh. "That one is going to be a down payment on my new car." He chuckled. "You've got that soulful look and that cute little wussy curl in your hair. I bet the advertising people at the Polo clothing line would love you. It would be better than zipping around in those rinky-dink planes. I wish to hell my dad had never taught you to fly." Mo had a distinct dislike for airplanes.

I shook my head. "Hey, I learned from the best! Chaz had all that experience in Vietnam and then flying for the doctors in Africa. You wouldn't be here if he hadn't flown to Zimbabwe and seduced your mom. Didn't she come out to the mission to help with the

AIDS situation?"

"Yeah, I guess. But she is still doing her paediatric practice part-time," Morris replied.

I laughed. "You would be sitting in the Nata Reserve, swirling Chibuku beer, ten kids running barefoot in the dirt, and working as a gardener or something if they hadn't adopted you."

"Fuck you," Mo said, grinning. "You would have been put in some dilapidated orphanage when your parents were killed and grown up with nothing else to talk about other than the Boerewors you were going to braai on a Saturday night, and who was going to win some stupid cricket match and how life used to be so great in the good old days when we---blah blah blah. You're lucky your Aunt Maggie rescued you and took you to South Africa."

"Well, that was before I found out who my dad really is," I said gruffly. I turned from Morris and walked towards the window and looked at the traffic and high-rise apartments. "Crazy to think about how we ended up here in California, isn't it?"

I looked at Morris. It was hard to read any emotion in his dark eyes. We were both quiet. With any other person, the talk of my parents would have seemed cruel, but Mo and I had shared so much over the years. Born in Zimbabwe. Lost our birth parents, or so I had thought. Brought up by couples that had come together by, was it fate? Chaz from Nashville; Sugar from Jamaica; Maggie from Zimbabwe; Bento from Portugal. And for good measure, a dad I had not known about. I shook my head and smiled. Hell, this would make a great movie!

## 20. Mo's Gig

I could tell by the way he sauntered out that the interview had gone well. I had gone with Mo to the Burbank office and sat in the elegant waiting room while the top producer at the film company gave him the once over. It was amazing that Morris had arrived in Los Angeles at eighteen, fresh out of high school in Nashville, and in three years had landed several top commercials and two pretty good roles in film. He hadn't been afraid to keep pushing, interviewing, and getting turned down. He had a happy, positive attitude and he kept showing up. Now, it seemed, it was starting to pay off.

Mo, dressed in a pair of tightly fitted jeans, black t-shirt and his signature black cowboy boots, had come out grinning. "My friend, you are going to crack up when you hear this one!"

I stood up and we started walking towards the exit door. "Well? You've got a lead role or what?"

He stopped and turned towards me, thrust his arms out to the side as if holding something large in each of them. He wrinkled up his face in a ferocious snarl, gave a blood-curdling cry and shouted, "Bayete, bayete!"

"Jeez, Mo. You gone nuts or something?"

He cracked up laughing and clasped me around the shoulders.

"Shamwari, we are going back to our roots. Africa calls. It's not official. One more interview, but I know it's in the bag. I've got this feeling again and I've been right every time."

We had walked to the BMW he drove and as he opened it he said, "You are looking at the next Great King. And, if you are lucky, you can come along as my escort."

"You really have lost it Mo. What the heck you on about!"

"The lead in the biggest movie the studio has done in years. Co-stars with names everyone knows and the filming is on location. They are doing the saga of the Zulu nation during the white take over and I'm in the running for Shaka Zulu!"

"You're kidding me." I started to laugh. "You going to ditch your Nashville twang? This should be great. Where they going to film? In some compound in the bush?"

"Laugh all you like. I get this, and I'll be laughing all the way to the bank. My new apartment will be a penthouse with an ocean view. And you, if you are smart enough, will apply for one of the charter pilots they will need." He turned the key and the motor purred.

He stopped with his hands on the wheel and looked towards me and quietly said, "I want to get this Sammy. The Zulu blood is in my veins. I know that my birth family was related to Chief Gambo, who was a descendant of the great Shaka Zulu." He was silent and I waited for him to speak. "I feel the presence of my ancestors. I know that their story should be told. Perhaps I can in some way honour my past."

He looked at me and in his dark eyes, I saw a flicker of sadness-- the baby that had been abandoned; the young boy who, despite having been adopted by a loving mother and father, had grown up far from his place of birth, his culture, and his heritage. He knew no traditions, could not speak the language of his tribe, and had no relatives that could teach him. He had gained in many ways, yet lost a whole world. He too, felt it; the distance between the land of our births and the place we now called home. We both had not been able to bridge the gap.

"I thought you had no clue about your native culture. I probably know more about it than you. Where did you learn about the Zulu war cry, Bayete?" I asked.

Morris grinned. "I just looked it up it, you dumb ass." He gunned the engine and pulled into the dense Los Angeles traffic.

## 21. Farewell

I had gone back to Carpinteria, back to my trailer in the foothills, but I was so unsettled.  Tanya and I had met for a conversation before I left Los Angeles and it was clear that it was time to call it quits.  Shoot!  This one didn't even last six months.  I sat on the deck of the trailer watching the fog roll in.  It had been gloomy for the past several days.

The phone rang and I smiled.  It was Avo.  He was up for a walk on the beach.  Maggie was at his house and would bring him to the trailer if I could give him a ride back to Santa Barbara after our visit.  He had not been able to renew his driver's license last month; at eighty-three he was starting to need more help and he didn't like it very much.

I met Maggie and Avo at Rincon Beach.  She and Bento were busy renovating their house and driving Sophia, who just had her 14th birthday, to and from school and numerous activities.  But Maggie was fit and happy, and I was grateful for that.

A few waves were rolling in as Avo and I strolled along the beach.  I hadn't seen him for a few weeks and was shocked at the way he had aged.  He shuffled along with his head bent down and his whole presence seemed to have shrunk into a now frail body. He had cut his hair and without the ponytail, it looked thin and receding. We spent an hour watching the surfers, most of the time sitting on the rocks and, thankfully, the sun had started to break through. He greeted many of the guys by name and they all took a moment to say hello and give high fives.

I drove back to the trailer and made some tacos, but Avo ate little and was content to lounge on the deck.

"We did a great job on this didn't we?" Avo commented, looking at the wrap-around wooden deck.

I smiled. "Yeah, I had a good supervisor."

Avo had given me the down payment for the trailer and had spent many hours with me as I worked on the landscaping and fixing up the property. Five years ago he had been up to some pounding of nails and working in the garden. That wasn't going to happen again.

"So," he said, "You still racking up so many hours at work?"

"Yeah, I take the overtime when I can. I don't know Avo, when I'm flying it seems to be the only time my mind is at ease. I love the ocean too, but when I'm in the plane I have to focus on what I'm doing and my mind clears. I feel free up there."

"Well, don't let it consume you, my boy. You have to find that balance. You can't expect to form a great relationship and be present with people if you don't create that time too." He winked at me and I saw the sparkle in his eyes was still there.

"That's something that seems to have eluded me so far," I muttered.

"You have to keep moving forward, Sammy. Learn from each encounter. That Tanya girl was nice, but I didn't feel you two were meant for each other, quite frankly." He paused and gazed towards the ocean. "What news of Peter?"

I looked at him, surprised that he had brought up Peter's name. I cleared my throat. "I haven't heard much. I guess he is doing okay. He was able to go back to a part-time job after the stroke. You know he was in rehab for a while, but he was lucky I guess. Didn't lose the use of his limbs and is a little slower, but is functioning and seems to have his life in order again. Maggie checks in with him now and again."

There was a break in our conversation. Then Avo propped himself up in the chair. "Did you ever have the conversation with him, Sammy? That you knew he was your father?"

I could feel my heart racing uncomfortably. I was in the hot seat again. Avo had this way of diving into subjects that I tried to push aside.

"No. When Maggie told me, Peter was still in a coma and I had to leave South Africa."

"You chose to leave." Avo threw in.

I bit my lip. "Alright, I chose to leave. I had things to take care of, but I guess I could have stayed if I had wanted to. I didn't want to accept it, Avo. I wasn't ready to deal with it."

"And now? It's been five years Sammy. Are you ready to acknowledge that man as your father, because my friend, like it or not, he is. I have this feeling that your life will become much smoother and you will find more joy if you can accept what is so, and bridge that gap between you." He paused and looked me with those unusually coloured eyes. "Both of you deserve that." He reached over and placed his hand over mine. "Don't leave it too late. Don't let that anger and pride stop you. It takes some effort to break through those old hurts and patterns, but it will be the biggest gift you can give yourself." He fell silent and his eyes closed.

I thought he had fallen asleep but after a few minutes, he stirred and said. "Hmmm. The sun feels good on these old bones, but it's getting late. Can you drive this old geezer? Oh, and by the way. I'd like you to take over the Kombi. That old gal needs a little TLC herself." He took one last look around the property and smiled. "You've done a great job here, Sammy. Keep up the good work."

"Well, it's all because of you, Avo. I could never have had this without your help. Giving me the down payment and…."

He held up his hand to stop me, shook his head and just smiled. He stood up slowly and took a few steps forward. I stood up to help him and he gave me a hug. He felt so thin.

"Now," he said, "it's time for me to go home."

* * *

I never saw Avo again. I had a two-week stint of flights to San Francisco and then flying some big wigs to and from Los Angeles. I had just landed in Santa Barbara on that Sunday evening when I got the call. Bento had left a message earlier that afternoon asking me to call him as soon as I could.  I signed off my roster and went to pick up my Jeep in the car park.  Before I drove off, I had called Bento. When he answered the phone I knew that he was upset.  His usual cheerful greeting was subdued.

"He has gone, Sammy.  My Pai has gone."

I steadied myself against the wall with one hand.  "Where are you, Bento?  I can come over right away."

"We are at his house.  Yes, come now."

I didn't bother to ask any other questions.  "I'm on my way."

I drove quickly to the house and pulled up into the driveway.  I sat for a moment and noticed the paint peeling on the purple shutters and how the garden needed some care.  The Jacaranda tree was without its colourful blooms.  Maggie, Bento, and a few neighbours were sitting in the living room.  Bento stood up and came over to hug me.  I was slightly taller than him and he buried his head onto my shoulder.

"Meu Pai," he said in a choked voice.  I waited for him to continue.  "He went this morning to the beach.  I kept telling him he needed to have someone with him.  But you know he liked to be independent.  He went for a swim and went too far out.  Oh, Deus. He never came back."

I could hear his gentle sobs and just held him.  I looked up and caught Maggie's eye as she sat gazing at us.  I closed my eyes.  I couldn't imagine Bento's pain.  I could not relate to his grief.  My father had nearly died and I had not been there for him.  I could not imagine weeping for him.

As I held his son, I could hear Avo's voice, "Don't let the anger and pride stop you."

I had let it affect me in so many ways.  I had been unable to open my heart fully to allow love in.  It had affected all my relationships. My mentor and friend was gone.

"Don't leave it until it is too late," he had said.

The evening light poured in through the large window and illuminated everything with a golden glow.  I could see the motes of dust in that beam of light.  It felt as if Avo was embracing Bento and me with his presence.  Compassion and regret rose through me. Bento squeezed me, lifted his head from my now damp shoulder, and stepped back.  He held my gaze as his dark eyes glinted with tears and amber sparkles.  I sighed.  There was nothing else to say.  As he walked away, I vowed it was time.  It was time to heal the past.

Later that evening Bento had gone to meet with the lifeguards and the police.  There had been no sign of Avo's body.  Maggie and I sat on his deck and she told me they suspected that Avo had swum away to freedom.  He had left no note, nor had he ever hinted that there was anything amiss, but going through his desk drawer they found results of tests, which showed an aggressive colon cancer.  He had told no one.  All his paperwork for the house and Kombi, life insurance, and Will were placed in an envelope in the same drawer, easily accessible.

"It was almost as if he was letting me know, Maggie.  The last time I saw him, he shared his heart with me.  Basically, he told me to get my act together.  His last words were, "It's time for me to go home.""

"Knowing Avo, he would have hated having to go through any treatment, or have us deal with his illness, but damn I'm going to miss him so much Sammy," Maggie said in a soft voice.  "He welcomed us with open arms.  I couldn't have asked for a better father-in-law."

It was tense for everyone in those first few days, as with each phone call we would wonder if there had been any news about Avo.  Was there the slightest possibility that he was still alive?  Could he have washed up on a beach down the coast?

Two weeks later Bento, Maggie, Sophia, and I took a day off.  The chances of his survival were minimum and we felt we needed some closure.  We took sprigs of bougainvillea from his garden and went to his favourite beach.  It was a bright, beautiful Santa Barbara day and the waves were putting on a show especially for him.  We scattered the blossoms of red, and purple over the ocean and each said our thanks for what he had contributed to our lives.  We went back to the house where his close friends and neighbours gathered and we celebrated and told stories of his life.  There was music with laughter and lots of Mexican food.  I think Avo would have enjoyed that party.

* * *

After two months we organized another day to remember Avo.  The local surfing groups came together and gathered at the beach below the University. There were old dudes with their longboards. Young teens and the in-betweens were all there to honour a well-known teacher and local hero. Many of the students and faculty from the University of California Santa Barbara were there. My avo, Jeffrey, had been on numerous charity boards and had spent his retired years helping at youth groups and soup kitchens. After Bento had said a few words of thanks to the community, many of us paddled out on surfboards. Bento and Sophia even came out as well. A circle was formed on the beautifully calm sea. I felt a deep appreciation for the time Avo had spent with me, and the way he had taken me under his wing.

The Chumash elder who had been his friend said a blessing and we scattered rose petals. As we paddled back, the circle of petals floated on the unusually turquoise water. The seagulls called a greeting as they soared high above. A shout from the beach had us cease our paddling to look back. The playful cavorting of a pod of dolphins in the middle of the rose circle had everyone cheering and laughing. They jumped and frolicked with graceful ease. They had come to give an exuberant farewell to Jeffrey/Avo.

## 22. Glimpses of the Past

Morris had talked about 'honouring his roots.' I had vowed to heal the past. It was time to go back to Africa; to go back to the Nata Reserve and then, to meet with my father. Losing Avo had made me realize that I needed to carry through with that promise.

I had been accepted as part of a flight crew by the studio. Morris and I decided to fly out two weeks before we had to report onsite in South Africa. I had cleared with my boss at Sun Coast Aviation to take an extended leave of absence. Maggie and Bento were going to check on the trailer and cars for me.

I met Bento on the patio of our favourite restaurant on Santa Claus Lane in Carpinteria. A fountain added a soothing touch and the birds flying to and fro were chirping happily. A few locals and some ritzy looking couples escaping the heat of Los Angeles, were sipping on lattes. Bento was sitting at the wooden table looking at the menu. He was dressed, as usual, in a casual but elegant way with a dark blue silk shirt and tan trousers. His thick hair was showing a few silver strands. I noticed that he had new glasses, but even with those, he seemed to be having difficulty reading.

"Sam, my son. Bom dia! You ready for your big trip?" He smiled as I settled in the seat across from him. He took off his glasses and rubbed his eyes. "How I wish I were going back with you. But this is a journey to undertake alone--a kind of ritual rite of passage--of homecoming. This will be both gratifying and I'm sure, at times, most uncomfortable for you." He reached out and laid his large hand over mine. "Come now. Order what you like. If I can remember, the food in Zimbabwe is not going to be quite what we have grown used to here."

We scanned the menu and placed our orders.

"You know Bento, I always wanted to ask you about your mother. I never really heard you or Avo mention that much about her," I said.

He clasped his hands together and was silent for a moment. "Well now. Mãe was quite a force to be reckoned with. She was feisty and sometimes opinionated and would give poor Avo a piece of her mind, but he loved her so. She was creative and very involved in the community. She and Avo moved back to Portugal after her exchange program in the USA. They were so young and it was a struggle for them both I'm sure, as I came along very soon after they were married. They had a wonderful life, but Mãe left us too soon. I was only ten when she died. It was some rare form of cancer that took her so quickly. Avo and I battled on, but he wanted to go back to the States. It just wasn't his home without her."

"But you had her family there, right?" I started to tuck into the burger that had been delivered.

Bento nodded, his mouth full of Caesar salad. "We had lots of aunts, uncles, and cousins, and my grandmother, who Sophia is named after, was still alive at that time."

"Didn't Maggie's grandfather and your grandmother know each other? I thought Maggie said something about that a long time ago. I remember asking why you had a picture of her grandfather in your study. The young man with the badza in his hand."

Bento smiled. "Yes. They met in Plumtree when your great-grandfather first arrived in Africa. 1914, I think it was. They had what you might call a bit of a fling and Grandmother painted the picture. She brought it back to Portugal." He paused to sip his water. "I think she never did forget the good looking young Englishman, Simon, but, as was expected of her, she married a nice Portuguese man and settled down." He gazed at the cool water bubbling in the fountain. "So strange how fate had a role in intertwining our families, isn't it Sammy?" He looked up and beamed as he saw Maggie and Sophia enter the patio.

He stood up and went towards them, kissing them both. He pulled two chairs towards the table and helped both of them sit down. I could do with emulating his manners. Perhaps I would have a girl stick around a little longer.

Sophia had joined us between her play rehearsals. I hadn't noticed how, in her teenage years, she was growing into a beautiful young woman. She had Bento's dark, luxurious hair and honey gold complexion, and Maggie's green eyes with dark lashes and dimples, which added to her beauty. They both ordered sparkling water and we chatted for a while.

"You keep yourself out of trouble Fi-Fi." I grinned at her. "And I want a full report on any prospective boyfriends, okay?"

"Huh, you can talk, Samson. I'm going to have to give YOU the okay for the next girl you date." Her long, curly hair bounced in waves as she tossed her head back.

Bento and Maggie laughed. "You two are going to be headaches for us, surely so," Bento said, winking at Maggie. It felt good to laugh with my family.

* * *

The next day Maggie picked me up at the trailer to take me to the airport shuttle at the shopping centre in Carpinteria. She sat on the deck while I finished closing up and when I had loaded my bags into her car I perched on the chair next to her.

"You ready?" She asked.

"Got all I can fit in… electrical adapters for my cell phone, if I can even get reception there."

She laughed. "I have no idea what the mobile phone reception is like. Didn't have to worry about that when I was last there. They didn't exist then."

"Do you wish you could visit again, Maggie?" I asked. I noticed the grey streaks in her hair and the little laugh lines around her eyes.

She took a deep breath. "I don't know Sammy. I don't know if it would be a good thing or not. There was so much pain and sadness, yet joy and finding new happiness all mixed up when I was last there that…." She sighed. "I think it is good that you and Morris are going. I think it will help to settle the past for you."

I gazed out at the sea. The wind had picked up and white caps dotted the ocean. "Do you ever wonder why I wasn't killed with James and Mom, why I was spared? What made Mom take me to my friend's farm that weekend?"

Maggie gave me an intense look and her eyes opened wider. "I don't know Sammy. Could your mom have had any kind of intuition that something was going to happen? I spoke to her a few weeks before and she seemed happy and content." She gave a slight grin. "You were just probably bugging her enough, that she needed a break." Her face softened as she said, "I can only be grateful that you were spared."

"You never really spoke about being with Mom in the hospital. Were you with her when she died?" I asked.

She bit her lip. "Do you really want to know?"

I nodded.

"James died on the farm. When that gang of Africans attacked he was struck with a badza on the head and was left there till the District Commissioner found him and Shelly. She was alive, but barely. God alone knows what had happened to her." The silence stretched out. "I got a call from Auntie Flo in Zimbabwe. I remember it was early in the morning. She asked me to come back from Canada. I flew back as soon as I could. You were still with Ruth and her kids. When I saw Shelly she was in a coma in the Bulawayo Hospital."

Maggie clasped her hands in her lap and her voice grew softer. "I walked into her room and she was hooked up to all these machines and she looked so broken and…. Well, I think it was a couple of days, I really can't remember, but I was called in because she had regained consciousness."

Maggie's gaze was off into the distance, into the past that she had tried to put aside. I think she had forgotten I was there.

"Shelly opened her eyes and she knew I was there. I can remember what she said: 'Sammy, my baby, he is a good boy. Tell him I love him--will always love him.' She looked up at me. She asked me to take care of you. She wanted me to promise to look after you."

I noticed I was holding my breath as Maggie said, "She made me promise! Pinkie swear."

Maggie's hands came closer to one another. She hooked her little fingers together. "Pinkie swear," she whispered in a hoarse voice.

## 23. Back to Our Roots

I caught the bus to Los Angeles where I met Mo at the airport. We sat in the LAX terminal waiting as our plane had been delayed. We both were quiet and I was reminiscing about my last two romantic relationships.

Then Morris asked, "Hey, do you think my mom and dad knew about Peter being your father? I know they all knew each other when they were working at the Methodist Mission, and when we all visited you guys in South Africa."

He was looking at me intently. Mo could go from totally serious to clowning around in a second. "I can't imagine my dad standing by and letting Peter treat you the way he did when you were a kid."

I laughed. "I don't know who would have beaten the crap out of him more, Chaz or your mom."

"Mom, for sure." Morris nodded his head with a smile on his face.

I looked up at him. "I don't think anyone else knew, except Maggie and Peter. You know, if I think about it, Peter was on the verge of telling me a few times as I was growing up. I'm just not sure why he didn't.  I guess I was totally like an ostrich; head buried so I wouldn't see what was right in front of me."

"Head up your backside more like it."  Morris grinned then turned serious again.  "Does he know you plan to visit?"

The loudspeaker blared on, announcing the flight time.  We still had to get through security.

"No, I haven't contacted him yet.  I guess when we get to the Mission and see how long we want to be there, I'll let him know."

"Yep, not sure how long I should be hanging out there."  Morris stood up and added, "I've got a load of scripts I have to go through and they want me to keep up with my physical training.  They want me sweating it out at the gym to beef up."

He flexed his arms.  The two cute young ladies sitting across from us started giggling and one took out her camera and shot a picture.  Morris smiled broadly, turned himself sidewise, and flexed again.  He gave a wink and blew a kiss.

"God Mo, you just lap it up, don't you?  Sure you don't want to give them an autograph now before you really are famous?"

He turned, flung his black leather jacket over his shoulder, grabbed his Louis Vuitton bag and sauntered away, giving me the finger as he did so.  I chuckled as I followed him, hauling my hand-me-down suitcase towards the long line at security.

* * *

We had a seven-hour stopover in Heathrow.  The South African Airways flight was on time.  I was excited about going back to Africa, and the new job; the film company had paid for the trip.  I chuckled to myself, as I watched the passengers board the plane.  Yup, I was heading back to Suid Afrika!  There were a bunch of kids in smart school uniforms, politely helping the older folks with their luggage.  There were a couple of khaki-clad, beefy-faced men, who had to be farmers.  Their veldskoens, farmer's tans, and accents gave them away.  I noticed some of the older women were dressed in elegant clothes, complete with stockings and dress shoes.  In contrast, the American tourists with their loud, casual conversation were clothed in slops, denims, and t-shirts.

I was noticing the cultural differences and wondered if I had changed that much since I had been living in the States.  I was never quite sure how to explain where I was from when people asked; Zimbabwe, South Africa, America?  I was a mixed bag; a mixed-up bag, for sure!

## 24. Ingwezi

Morris and I arrived in Zimbabwe.  After picking up a rental car at the airport in Harare, we had many miles and hours to contemplate our lives as we headed for Bulawayo.  Although I had been in Africa from birth to eleven years old, I had not gone back to the farm where Mom and James had been killed.

Once we were out of Harare, there were miles and miles of open countryside.  How different from where we were living in California.  Chaz had brought Morris back to Zimbabwe when he was fifteen but, he too had never been back to Matabeleland where he had been born.  We had made good time and by late afternoon had checked into the Churchill Hotel in Bulawayo.  We were both tired but refreshed ourselves with a dip in the pool.  Morris had a way of making friends and chatting with people easily.

The two smiling waiters who served us dinner would not believe that Morris was born in Matabeleland.  Morris started asking them to give him some basic Sindebele phrases.  I laughed when he started recording the video of the waiters.  This was going to be an interesting trip.  We called it a night and were asleep before ten.

The dark curtains had blocked out the morning sun and we had decided not to set an alarm.  After all, we were on holiday.  Morris woke me up singing in the shower and by the time we went to the dining room it was last call for breakfast.  Since there were few people in the room, we got excellent service.  The memories from long ago started to surface, as I smelled the aroma of the traditional English breakfast--fried eggs, fried bread, sausage, and tomatoes.  We powered down a mountain of food and then sat on the veranda finishing a second cup of coffee.

We had contacted the Ingwezi School while we had been in the U.S.  There were many advantages of searching the Internet.  I had told them that my great-grandfather, Reverend Simon Morris, had founded the school and that Morris had been born there.  I was told that the "mission" as such was no longer operating but the school had taken over the house for staff quarters and the chapel was used only on special occasions.  The Children's Centre where Morris had been as a baby and was started by one of the Ministers for the orphans in the area, was no longer in operation.  The senior prefects now used those rooms.  We had been assured of accommodation while we were there.

We left Bulawayo midday and travelled the two hours to the small town of Plumtree.  We didn't stop except to fill up with fuel.  I had this strange feeling as we travelled closer and closer to Ingwezi.  It felt as if I was looking through the lens of a camera but someone else was viewing the scene as it was being recorded--flashes of colour, the tawny sweep of long grasses swaying in the wind, the brittle dark of a thorn tree trunk.  There was an intense flash of sunlight bouncing off a metal roof as we whizzed by an empty farmhouse.  Morris was lost in his own thoughts.  For me, a welling up of anticipation was layered with a blanket of nostalgic memories.

It was mid-afternoon by the time we had bounced and rattled over the dusty road and pulled up to a large gate.  Above the gate was a wrought iron sign: Ingwezi Mission.  Since Morris was driving, I jumped out to swing open the wide gate.  I had done that so many times as a young child.  Down the road there were a few buildings and, if I remembered correctly, the chapel.  Morris pulled forward and I swung the gate firmly shut, hearing my mother's voice reminding me to fasten it securely so that the goats and scrawny cows would not escape.

We drove slowly up the road, the dust billowing behind us.  We parked in front of what we had called 'the office.' There was a wide veranda in front and an old rocking chair, where the kindly Minister Frank, who had seemed ancient to me at six years old, liked to sit and doze in the sun. The giant marula tree was still there with its huge branches reaching out to bring a cooling pool of shade beneath them.

The screen door opened and a young African woman came out. She was dressed in a colourful skirt and plain blouse, with leather sandals on her feet. Her hair was woven into tight braids. I guessed she was in her mid-thirties.

"Hello, hello. Welcome to Ingwezi." She smiled.

I walked forward. "I'm Sam Morris. Hello." I held out my hand for her to shake.

She stopped and her mouth dropped open. "Little Sammy? Ikona!" She shook her head and I thought she was about to cry. She grabbed me and pulled me into a hug. I had no idea who she was.

Morris stepped forward with a grin on his face, obviously enjoying my dazed expression. "Howdy, Ma'am. I'm Morris Jackson."

At that, the lady threw her hands over her mouth and gave a cry. It was hard to tell if it was delight or anguish.

We looked at each other then Morris opened his arms wide and said to her, "Well you better give me a hug then, too, whoever you are!" Morris towered above her and gave me a wink as he embraced her.

"Oh, I'm so sorry," the lady said, letting go of Morris. "It's just such a huge shock to see you both. I am a teacher here at the school. My name is Victoria."

Victoria, Victoria. I knew that name. "Victoria?"

"Yes Sammy, you were just a little boy and used to play with us in the Children's Centre when your mother was helping Frank in the office. Then, I couldn't play with you so much because...." she stopped and turned towards Morris, "...there was this cheeky little baby that I had to look after."

"Oh my God! You were baby Morris!" I gazed at the towering man beside me. "Victoria toted you around for hours on end. I never put the pieces together." I laughed out loud. "I remember you as this chubby little baby that everyone wanted to hold AND I remember the day Chaz and your Mom got engaged."

"Oh my, my," Victoria chimed in. "Yes, Chaz and Sugar. I baked them this cake that didn't turn out so well. I must have been about thirteen and not very good in the kitchen." She gave a chuckle and then her features seem to soften. "But they managed to take you away to America. I was sad for a long time." She gazed at Morris with tenderness. "And look at you now!"

The next few days were filled with a kaleidoscope of memories. The building we were in hadn't changed since I was 6 years old--solid brick walls and metal roof. The living room had the same old lumpy armchairs and piano that badly needed a tuning. I showed Morris the picture of my great-grandfather, Simon, that still hung on the wall.

"Sure is a family resemblance," he said. "But your great-grandpa was a good looker. What happened to you? "

I slapped him on the arm. We ended up sleeping in the room that my mom and I had always used when we stayed overnight while James was away from the farm. The twin beds were way too small for Morris and me, but the price was right.

As I showed Morris around the grounds we settled into a deeper connection. He had only been a baby when Chaz and Sugar had adopted him and taken him to Nashville, so he had no recollections of the place or people, but perhaps it was a soul memory that bonded us more intimately.

We walked to the chapel, which was in need of a fresh coat of whitewash. The garden in front of it needed tending too. Avo came to mind when I saw the poor neglected bougainvillea. He would have loved to put on his thick leather gloves and give it a good tending to.

I pushed the heavy door of the chapel and it creaked open. A still, expansive presence seemed to fill the space. Our footprints stood out on the red film of dirt on the cement floor as we walked quietly inside. Everything was covered in a fine coating of dust; the benches of heavy wood, the pulpit, and the altar. Instinctively my gaze was drawn upward. The beautiful stained glass window that I had loved to gaze at while sitting in the Sunday service was still there. Yes, my friend the mourning dove was still flying free! Her white wings were spread as if flying on a golden beam of light. I silently greeted her and felt my heart burst open.

Morris and I stood paused in thought. This simple building held the essence of love and compassion, of healing and of faith. All those things that Morris and I yearned for. It was as if our ancestors were anointing us with their energy.

I could hear Maggie's voice as she repeated to me the words her grandfather had shared with her as a child, "Never be afraid to do what is right.  Your voice is important.  Hamba lami.  Go with me, God."

We left the chapel and walked quietly, pausing at the old cemetery where we sat on the red-rusted iron bench.  We sat silently.  No radio or television to disturb us.  No phone to answer, or internet to check.  We were content to be--for a few minutes.

Then Morris stood up and said,  "Okay tour guide, that was cool, now where is the Supreme Scream rollercoaster ride?"

I laughed and stood up.  "Fresh out of excitement for a few more days, Mo!"

* * *

We walked over to the school.  It was still supported by the Methodist Church, but like most things in Zimbabwe, there was always a shortage of supplies and everything needed a little TLC and a fresh coat of paint.  The students, though, were dressed in uniforms and were thrilled to have visitors to the school.  The Headmaster treated us as special guests and the next morning we were invited to attend Assembly.  My great-grandfather, Reverend Simon Morris and his constant helper, Mo's great-grandfather, Pile, were acknowledged for starting the school in 1922 with a couple of classrooms.  I felt like a celebrity standing in front of hundreds of kids who clapped and clapped and sang for us and greeted us with such enthusiasm.  To them, this school was a lifesaver and the only hope they had of creating a better future.  To me, it had been something from my past that I had never thought about after I moved away.

I had stored away those memories of my life as a young boy on the Nata Reserve.  If some remembrance had risen up, it always felt as if a part of my heart and been slightly shredded.  Now I regretted that I had not kept those ties and wished I had taken more interest in the family history.

The hardest part of our visit was when we went back to the farm. It was about forty-five minutes from the school and Morris and I went back on Saturday afternoon.  I had been told that it had been taken over for a time by a group of squatters, probably those that had killed my family.  Then, during a period of drought when the water supply was almost non-existent, it had been abandoned and stripped of anything of value. I had a hard time recalling the directions, even though one of the teachers had drawn me a map. The only thing I recognized was the bend in the road that veered off towards the dam where James and I had spent many hours fishing for barbel. The land was barren. No crops had been planted and there was no livestock roaming the fields. I had to fight back a wave of sadness as I saw the farmhouse. The metal roof had been stripped. All the doors had been taken. A few of the window frames had been pried out. It felt as if the house was looking at me with sightless eyes and a mouth gaping with horror. There were a couple of bed frames left and the huge old kitchen table that would have taken a bulldozer to move. Everything else including light fixtures, water tanks, the old wood stove in the kitchen, and the doors from the cupboards had been taken. I wandered through the rooms but the bleak, empty space held nothing but sorrow.

After about fifteen minutes I called out to Morris, who was sitting on the steps leading down to what had been a beautiful garden. "I'm done. Let's get the hell out of here!"

We drove away. I did not look back.

"You know, I think that after we visit what's left of my family tomorrow, we should head back to civilization," Morris said.

I nodded my head in agreement.

## 25. Meeting the Matabele

I asked Mo if he wanted me to come with him when he met his cousin.

"Hell yes," he replied, "I definitely need some back up on this one. Not so sure this was such a great idea, my friend. After seeing that freakin' farm, perhaps leaving things in the past is a better plan."

His mom had died when he was six months old. No one had confirmed, but we both thought it was from AIDS. His father had left and it was presumed he had gone to South Africa, but Morris did not know his name and had not wanted to try and trace him. All he knew was that his great-grandfather, Pile, had been on the Mission with Simon Morris and, as a Matabele, he had some connection to the last great leader, Chief Gambo.

Although his cousin lived off the reserve, we were going to meet at the kraal where his aunt still lived. I think we were both nervous and, once again, I was overcome by the richness of our lives in America. I noticed that we both wore old shorts and well-worn shirts. Mo took off his expensive watch and the thick gold chain he usually wore around his neck.

It was just a short walk down a rugged old trail to the collection of huts that housed some of the Africans that worked at the school and on the school farm. Some brick buildings had been built, but many still lived in the traditional round huts built of wooden poles and topped with thatched roofs. The déjà vu feelings returned. I had spent time at the kraal with my friends, the herd boys. We would go back to their huts and have a lunch of sadza and stew after Mama had given us our lessons in counting and writing with sticks in the dusty ground. I found myself remembering some of the songs we would sing, and some of the Sindebele words.

As we walked towards the fork in the path and veered to the left, a man who had been sitting outside one of the huts stood up and came towards us. He was tall and dressed in a short-sleeved cotton shirt and long trousers. His face was a rich chocolate colour and he greeted us with a big smile.

"Kanjani." He held out his hand to Morris. They shook hands firmly and looked at each other intently. He turned to me and greeted me. "My name is Solomon."

He led us towards the hut where an African lady sat outside on a wooden chair. She had on a simple dress; I remember it was bright yellow. Her face was lined with wrinkles, although she did not have much grey in her hair. She was slim and sat upright with her back straight, and her eyes were closed as if she were resting.

Solomon spoke to her rapidly in Sindebele and then turned towards Morris. "Your mother's name was Thoko. This is her older sister, your auntie."

I could see beads of sweat forming on Morris's brow and he swallowed. He knelt in front of her and reached out his hands. She did not reach out for them and he laid them gently on her legs. She took them, then, in her hands. She reached forward and gently touched his face, slowly caressing his cheek. Her hands went to the top of his head and she stroked his hair. It was then that I realized she was blind.

"Ibizo lakho. What is your name?" she asked.

Solomon translated and helped Morris to answer in Sindebele. "My name is Morris, Auntie."

"Ahhh, so." She smiled. "You are called after the Mfundisi Morris. That is good." She sighed. "You are well, my son?"

"Yes, I am well, Auntie," Morris said softly.

We were invited to sit on a small wooden bench. Solomon told us about his bookkeeping company and his family; Morris had four second cousins. He told us that many other relatives had been killed in what they called the Matabele Massacre, Gukurahundi. He did not want to elaborate on the horrors that had occurred from 1983 to 1987.

The government, in a bid to keep 'dissidents' under control, slaughtered the Ndebele people. I realized that it was during the time we were on the farm, that these atrocities had occurred. We had been part of it. When Thoko had died and a brutal killing of several members of the family had occurred, Solomon and Auntie left Matabeleland. To escape the violence they moved to Harare, the capital city of Mashonaland. They had left baby Morris at the Mission, as they had no means to support the child. They had returned to their home in this area a few years ago. They were relieved to hear that Morris had the opportunity for a better life.

We could not converse with Auntie, who had never learned English, and Solomon had to leave so we stood up to say goodbye. His aunt spoke to Solomon, who ducked through the low door into the hut. He came back and placed something in her hand. She beckoned Morris towards her and again, he knelt down in front of her. She held out her hand and he grasped hers. Her wizened hand turned his strong one over and she placed an object into it. I could not see what it was.

"This was made by your mother," Solomon told Morris. "She was known in the area for her beautiful beadwork. She had just made contact with a lady who wanted to send her work overseas." He smiled as he said, "you were a baby and she would work with you tied onto her back, as she made her crafts. Soon she became too sick to do very much. Auntie asked her to make something special for her son to have when he was grown. She made this, and Auntie has kept it all these years, never knowing if she would ever have the chance to meet her nephew, or be able to give him the gift his mother made."

I moved closer and saw a beautiful beaded bracelet. It was made of the smallest glass beads in beautiful colours and intricate patterns. Auntie took Morris's wrist and gently fastened the bracelet on his arm. She laughed out loud, patting Morris's hand while she spoke.

Solomon laughed too, telling Morris that Thoko must have known her son would grow up to be a big, strong warrior. "She made the bracelet very large and it just fits you."

Morris seemed to be overwhelmed as he hugged Auntie.  There was not much more he could say besides goodbye.  He could not promise to return; to see them again; to share family time.

"Hambe kahle."  He said to her in a choked voice.

"Hambe kahle."  We heard echoed back, as we walked slowly and silently from that African kraal.

We had been there for less than an hour.  Had the Amadlozi, the spirits of the ancestors, been with us at that encounter?  The impact of that meeting had affected both of us; gifting us with power as great and forceful as the mighty Victoria Falls; the strength of the resilient boabab tree; the courage of a Matabele induna.

## 26. Possibility

I had called Peter and told him I would be in Durban in a few days; how my new job had allowed me to come back to Africa; how I had wanted to visit Ingwezi and the farm. He sounded pleased to hear from me and we had a good talk. I told him of the mixed emotions-- the happy memories that had surfaced and the pain that was still deeply embedded on other occasions. It was the first time that I felt he finally listened to me. Perhaps I was sharing from my heart more, and inviting him into the conversation by asking about some of his experiences. We ended up chatting for more than half an hour and I told him I was looking forward to seeing him. There was a moment of silence before he replied that he had been waiting for this for a long time. We had arranged that he would pick me up from Durban airport on Tuesday. It was an evening flight from Harare and I would get in at eleven o'clock.

Morris and I left Ingwezi together and drove back to Harare. He left on a flight to Johannesburg, where he had meetings with the producers before they went on to the filming location. As I sat in the airport lounge in Harare, I wondered if I would ever return to Zimbabwe. It felt as if that chapter of my life had finally been allowed to close.  Now, I had the opportunity to heal the chasm with Peter.  I was hopeful that after our telephone conversation, we would put to rest the painful history and be able to create some sort of future together, albeit it would probably be long distance.

My cell phone rang and I saw Peter's name flash on the screen.  I was in the middle of chowing down on a plate of steak and chips and, as I hadn't eaten all day, I let the phone ring.  I would call him back as soon as I was finished eating.  I had an hour to wait before the flight and I had a leisurely meal and got engrossed in a flight magazine.  It was almost forty-five minutes before I checked the phone to listen to the message that had been left.

"Sammy, my boy.  Why the hell you have to catch such a late bloody flight?  Got to keep myself occupied for another few hours now.  But don't you worry, I can probably do that alright!"  He gave a loud chuckle.  "I'll be there.  What was the flight number now?"

There was a blast of music and then my stomach contracted as I heard the unwanted and unforgotten sound of tinkling glasses and coarse laughter.

"I'm jusshed hanging out with a few mates.  Gotta go now."

I could hear the slur in his voice.  There was a crash and then the sound of voices rising and falling before the message ended.  The phone slipped from my hand onto the table.  I pushed my empty plates aside and cradled my head in my hands.

"Oh God, no," I mumbled, and then my fist slammed onto the table, the knife and fork clattering onto the floor.  "Dammit, Peter.  I don't believe this.  Back in the bloody pub."

I could feel the burn of anger, yet just below that was this immense well of sadness.  Perhaps there was still time to help him.  I reached for the phone and called him back.  It rang.  "Come on, come on, pick up!"

"Hello. This is Peter."  There was a pause and I was just about to talk when I realized it was his message.  "I'm busy right now, but I'll call you back."

"Peter, call me back right away.  It's really important.  I need to speak to you.  Please call."  I cradled the phone in my hands, willing it to ring.  "It's too late," I said to myself.

The tone of his voice--the mumble of his words--as a boy I had been able to judge how far down the road he had gone and that barometer was still in place.  I slowly put the phone on the table.  I sat staring ahead; the bubble of hope and happiness had deflated. I knew he was not going to call back.

* * *

I boarded the plane with a heavy heart. All the hope that I had of being able to accept him as my father, of creating a relationship, had evaporated. As the hostess offered the beverages I was tempted to drown my sorrows; but no way was I going to have Peter, or was it the booze, win. I would not let that happen.

"Soda water. No ice. Lemon if you have it." I took the small plastic cup, my hand shaking a little as I did so. "Cheers and damn you, Peter," I muttered.

* * *

As I expected, there was no one to meet me at Durban airport. I took an Uber to a small motel close to where we had lived. I tried to call again, but Peter did not pick up. I could not settle and eventually called my Uber friend again. I asked him to drive me to the country club. That road to the clubhouse held so many uncomfortable memories. My stomach was roiling with emotion. It was after midnight. I walked back into that smoke-filled, noisy bar and my heart plummeted. There was still a crowd of people there, but there was no sign of Peter. I knew no one there and the bartender, who was not my old friend Phineas, had no recollection of him. I went back to the motel and eventually managed to sleep, hoping that Peter was safe in his bed, sleeping it off.

The scene played out, as I knew it would. The next day, I waited at the motel. I had no idea where Peter lived as he had just moved. I tried to call the local hospital but they would not give me any information. I tried to call Maggie. The day seemed endless.

Later that evening there was a call from Maggie. Peter was in the hospital. The police had picked him up for speeding. He had been asked to take the breathalyser test and had started to argue and got belligerent and then had collapsed. The emergency crew had taken him to the hospital. They had not been able to identify him until, after several hours, they found his wallet hidden in his car. Maggie had been listed as the contact person. The police had only been able to reach her after several attempts due to the time difference in the States.

* * *

As I walked towards the hospital room where Peter lay, I started crying for my mom and James.  Why they had suffered so?  I didn't know.  Why had they died, so young?  Most of all I felt as if I was crying for what might have been--for a childhood with them that I hadn't had.

The memory of walking down a slick, antiseptic-smelling corridor assailed me and I wanted to turn and run.  I didn't want to see this man, my father.  This man who I had shielded myself from, emotionally and physically.  I wanted to confront him and make him suffer, as Mom and James had suffered--as Maggie had suffered.  He had caused so much heartache.  How could I love him?  How could I call him Dad?

## 27. A Spark of Light

I sat on the bench outside his room for a long time.  It was after eight o'clock in the evening.  I might have sat there and fallen asleep if it hadn't been for the night shift of nurses coming on duty.

A gentle hand touched my shoulder and roused me.  "If you are wanting to go in, you should go now.  We will be settling the patients for the night in a little while."

I looked up into the lightest blue eyes I had ever seen.  They were almost translucent and they seemed to look right through me.  I just sat dazed.

A smile crossed the young nurse's face.  "Are you a relative?"

I nodded, not trusting my voice.

"Well, I'm Nurse Justine.  I'm afraid it might be a shock to see him.  Would you like me to come in?"

I nodded again and stood up slowly.  Man, I must be tired.  My brain was all muddled and I could hardly walk.

"Justine," I whispered to myself as I followed her into the room.

She went over to the bed and checked some large machine that Peter was hooked up to, then stepped aside and waved me forward. He was lying with his face to one side and I noticed his mouth was all pulled up at the corner.  Drool trickled onto the paper bib that had

been placed around his neck.  His hair was silver-grey and his face
looked hollow and lined.  His eyes fluttered open and he coughed; a
loud, rattling sound.  The nurse went to the side of the bed and bent
down towards him.  She gently wiped his mouth.  I noticed her
delicate hands.

"There is someone here to see you."

There was no reply.  Then Peter moved very slowly, just his
fingers, beckoning me forward.  Justine nodded at me and moved to
one side.  I walked over and stood awkwardly looking down.  Peter
turned his head slightly and gazed at me.  He managed a hint of a
lopsided smile.  His eyes closed again.  I reached out and placed my
hand over his.  I felt his fingers curl slightly.

"My son," he croaked.

I swallowed.  I saw Justine turn her head to look at me.  Her
mouth was open in surprise.

"Yeah, it's Sam.  I'm here Dad," the words slipping out without
me thinking.

There was nothing else to say.  Those words: my son--Dad--had
bridged a gap so vast, from so long ago that everything else, at that
moment, melted away.  I just stood there cradling his hand,
wondering what had led this man to these circumstances; to be in this
condition at this time and place.

He fell back asleep.  I sat watching him for a while, remembering
him on those rare occasions when he seemed happy and when he had
tried to show me he cared.  He had never spoken to me about his
leaving Zimbabwe, or about what had occurred between my mom
and him.  I had never realized that he might have been in pain and
lonely too.

I went slowly from the room.  I sat back down on the bench.
After a few minutes, Justine came out.  I hadn't noticed how petite
she was.  Her silver-blond hair was tucked underneath the nurse's
cap.  She had a band of freckles across the bridge of her nose.

"It's late now and we ask all visitors to leave, but will you be
coming back?" she asked.

"Yes.  What time can I see him again?"

"Well, if you can be here fairly early, while I am on duty, there is
something I would like to give you.  Something that Mr Nell wanted
to share with you."

"Would eight be okay?"

"I'll just be getting off shift. Why don't you meet me at the café next door."

"Okay. That will work. And thank you."

She stood still for a moment and our eyes met, and then she walked away.

* * *

I had managed to fall into a deep sleep that night. I was glad I set my alarm. I would have missed the meeting with Justine. I showered quickly and then walked towards the hospital. It felt good to stretch my legs after the flight. On the next block, there was a row of shops and a small coffee shop tucked into an alley. I hoped this was the place Justine had been talking about. The courtyard was small and paved with slate, and pots of red geraniums brightened the space. Justine was sitting on the patio at a small wrought iron table reading what looked to be a paperback novel. An amazing aroma wafted towards me from a cup of coffee in front of her and I realized how hungry I was. The food on the plane was not all it was cracked up to be.

"Hi, Justine."

I was usually so bad with names, but I had not forgotten hers. She looked up and again I was stunned at the colour of her eyes. I noticed they were framed with dark lashes, which made them appear huge; the image of a beautiful fawn crossed my mind. I wondered if she was used to the attention she must get. She smiled and pushed the book aside. She was still dressed in her nurse's uniform and she looked a little tired herself.

"You look a little more rested than you did last night. I presume you are from America?" she asked.

"Yes, I was pretty thrashed, but how did you know where I've been living?"

"That accent of yours!" She laughed.

"I have an accent? You mean I have picked up a Yankee drawl? You are the one with the accent." I smiled. "Yours has a hint of South African, but there is something else mixed up in there."

"More pure Dutch than Afrikaans," she answered. I have only been here since I graduated high school."

"Can I get you anything? I need a Grande for sure."

She shook her head. "Go ahead. I'm fine. Dankie," she said with a grin.

I grabbed a coffee, no latte in this shop, and a couple of rusks, which were great to dunk. I hadn't had them in years. We chatted for a while. The conversation flowed easily. I told her about the many Dutch flower growers living in Carpinteria.

She expressed her concern when I shared why I was here, back in South Africa, because I had heard about Peter's condition. She was quietly sipping at her coffee.

"I hope you don't mind me asking, but I couldn't help but wonder how it was to see your dad like that. He was able to communicate when he was first admitted and it came out that he hasn't seen you for many years."

Was it her calm, welcoming presence that made me feel as if she genuinely cared? There was a resonance that flowed between us and I told her the whole complicated, messy story. She gazed at me with those all-knowing eyes, nodding occasionally and letting me download years of pain and disappointment. Our coffees grew cold. At one point she had reached over with her smooth, delicate fingers and stroked my hand and I had felt my heart flutter wildly. I told her about finding out that this man, Peter, was actually my father. She sighed, and her eyes were shining with tears. We must have been talking for at least an hour when she yawned and I realized she had been up all night.

"I'm an idiot. You should be heading home to sleep. I'm sorry I've kept you so long."

"I'm off for a couple of days. I can catch up. I really wanted you to see this." She pushed the book towards me and I saw that it was a thick notebook. "I want to let you know that I try not to get personally involved with my patients. It is just better that way." She gazed at me again. "When Peter came into our ward he was able to talk and move around a little. The stroke had affected the one side, but he was cognizant. I was on duty when he first came in and he started to talk to me about his life, what had happened. At one point he asked if I could do him a favour, in case his condition deteriorated. What could I say, but yes? He gave me this notebook and wanted me to take care of it. He didn't trust the hospital system. He wanted me to pass it on to his son. He said he was sure that his son would come to see him, but he had left two phone numbers scribbled on the inside cover."

Justine took a sip of the cold coffee and grimaced. I couldn't help but smile. There was a long pause.

"Peter had another stroke, just a few hours after he came in. He hasn't spoken, except for yesterday, when he saw you." She sat, her breath slow and deep. "I want you to take this now, so I have kept my promise to him."

I picked up the book and thumbed through it. It was a handwritten diary. The pages were worn and I noticed that the first entry was when we had arrived in South Africa in 1986. As I flipped the pages two photographs slipped onto the table. I picked them up slowly. I gazed at the first. My mom and Peter, young and gazing at each other with adoring faces, were framed against the backdrop of the Victoria Falls. I could feel my throat closing up. He looked as if he truly loved her. Mom had her head thrown back as if she were laughing out loud.

The second photo was of a toddler on a swing. It was an old metal swing in a playground. There was a big tree in the background. That kid was laughing up a storm too, legs flying out in front and looking as if he hadn't a care in the world. The man behind him, giving him a push, was Peter. I just stared at the photo. Peter and I in happier times.

A group of doctors in their white coats walked towards the counter.

"I have to go," Justine said.

"Of course. I'm sorry."

We both stood and she grabbed her handbag. I didn't know what to do. I didn't want her to go.

"Look, I know you have done more than enough for Peter and me, but…." I ran my hand through my hair. Damn did I always do that when I was nervous? "I will only be here another couple of days. Could I see you again? Buy you a dinner to say thanks?"

She smiled and her nose wrinkled, the freckles seeming to dance. "I guess you are not a patient, so I don't think I'm breaking any hospital protocol. Here's my card. If you have time, we can grab a quick bite."

As she started to walk away, she stopped and turned around, and said softly, "I'm sorry you weren't able to be with your dad before the second stroke."

## 28. The Final Meeting

For the next two days, I spent most of my time at Peter's side. He slept and had occasional moments of being aware of what was going on. I wasn't sure how much he could comprehend, but I spoke to him about the impact that his journal had on me. I had started reading it that first morning after Justine had shared it with me. I sat in the hospital room that held him hostage and learned of the softer, sweeter side of that man that I had hated so much. He wrote about his battle with alcohol. The times he was so clear that he was finished with it; he had it licked. But then the insidious way that it reached out slyly, and pulled him back into a deep, dark pool, where he became as he said, "a lesser version of who I am. A man I would not want to call my friend, a man I wouldn't want to call Father."

So he had kept the secret of being my father hidden until he felt he could be someone I would be proud to have in my life. The last quote in the book was written in an almost unreadable scrawl, written in pencil and I assumed, under the influence of his unwelcome companion, the night of his first stroke.

"It's too late. It's too late for Shelly, for Sammy, for me. I have failed us all. I have broken the promise I made to Shelly--to love her-

-to be there for her always.  I've no right to claim Sammy as mine; he deserves better.  You win.  The booze wins.  I've nothing else."

I sat stunned and saddened that the man I glimpsed in these writings was not the man I knew.  I cursed the booze--the addiction--for taking away what was rightfully mine, and my mom's--Peter's love.

* * *

The call came in the early hours of the morning.  The motel room was dark and I was startled awake.  I glanced at the cell phone before I answered the call.  It was just before five o'clock.

"May I speak to Sam Morris please?"

"This is Sam, who is calling?"  I could feel my heart beating.

"Mr Morris, this is Virginia.  I'm calling from the hospital."

As she took a breath, I knew what she was going to say.

"I'm sorry to have to inform you that your father passed away a short time ago.  We did all we could to save him, but he had another stroke and we could not resuscitate him."  There was silence.  "Will you be able to get to the hospital?"

"Yes, I'll be there as quickly as I can."  I ended the call.

I pulled back the curtains.  The glow of the rising sun was just beginning to shine its light and welcome another day.  I took in a breath as I viewed the splash of pinks and purple tinged with golden rust.

The words I had read yesterday echoed through me.  "It's too late. It's too late for Shelly, for Sammy, for me."

I dressed and walked outside.  The air was fresh.  Delivery trucks and those on the early crews were starting to drive, cycle, and walk to their normal day.  Newspaper boys tossed their rolled-up bundles. The coffee shop was just opening, and I stopped for a takeaway.  I took a sip.  It was hot and almost bitter--a strong brew this morning. I was going to need it, to get through this not-so-normal day.

* * *

It was late afternoon when I walked slowly from the hospital.  A random assortment of images filled my mind.  The body lying so still and yes, it seemed to me, at peace at last.  Some questions had to be answered, decisions to be made, and long phone conversations with Maggie who guided me through the uncomfortable time.  I had cleared with the studio to stay until the cremation at the end of the week.  Maggie had given me the address where Peter had been living, and I spent the next few days sorting and clearing his possessions.  His mom had passed and his sister in Australia was not able to come back.  Maggie was not coming back either.  It was a surreal time and the only bright light was Justine's warm smile.  We met on two different occasions and she, with her calming presence, was just the support I needed.

That Sunday a small gathering of acquaintances from his work and the apartment where he had been living, met together at the small park close by.  There were a few people from the local support group and even some of his older friends from his days at the club.  I asked the Pastor from the local church to say a few words, and he dropped by after the Sunday service, even though Peter had not been a regular member of his congregation.  I scattered some of his ashes at the park and after the get-together, I walked to the beach and allowed the waves to carry away the rest.  I was sad, but mostly for what seemed to me, a life that could have been so much more; sad for the unfulfilled dreams; sad for the unresolved heartaches.

## 29. Looking Forward

Justine came to say goodbye to me at the café. In a few hours, the charter company we would be partnering with was picking me up. I was flying to a private farm in the Free State, where the filming would take place.

I caught my breath as I saw her enter the café. Her pale blue dress was the exact colour of her eyes and her halo of silver-blond hair shimmered in the sunlight. I wanted to frame that picture of her in my mind. We spent an hour together and again, I felt the resonance and ease of being with her. Her tinkling laugh soothed my bruised heart. We said goodbye and as she reached up on tiptoe to kiss my cheek, I felt a flood of gratitude and tenderness wash through me. I closed my arms around her, afraid she would pull away, but she melted into the hug and we stayed in a serene embrace--tranquil and deeply connected. Slowly, I bent my head and as she looked up, I felt as if I was melting into her. Silky soft lips touched mine lightly and her eyes closed.

There was no need to do anything more, but receive her embrace. As she released me from her hold, there were no words spoken, but the unsaid was more profound than anything I had ever experienced.

I watched her walk away and it seemed that Africa had called me back to complete the past and perhaps open a doorway--a pathway-- leading into a brighter future.

30. Success
Santa Barbara, California  2013

"Fi-Fi, do me a favour and run upstairs and help Justine settle the kids.  They always love it when you tuck them into bed.  The red carpet parade is going to be on soon and we may catch a glimpse of Morris strutting his stuff."

"And why, my dear Samson, does the father lounge on the couch, while the auntie has to deal with the road rats?"  Sophia laughed at me.

"Well, who has been getting the house ready all day and setting up the giant plasma screen," I retorted.

She tossed her luxuriant hair over her shoulders as she ran lightly upstairs, giving me a beaming smile as she did so.  Sophia was in her second year at UCSB and as busy as she was, had graced us with her presence, this time without one of her handsome escorts.

The barking of the neighbour's dog alerted me to the arrival of visitors.  I looked out of the window and was pleased with the view of the garden below.

"How do you like what I've done with the fish pond, Avo?  I thought that you would approve of the waterfall."  I had many silent conversations with Avo.

We had moved into his house soon after Justine and I were

married.  Maggie and Bento were happy living in Carpinteria and, being in Santa Barbara, closer to the airport, was better for my work. I had built my own charter company into a good business, thanks to the contacts that I had those many years ago with the Hollywood crowd.  I employed two other pilots and that allowed me to take time to help Justine with the kids.  Tory at 4 and Bennie, just 2 now, kept us on our toes.

My heart melted a little as I watched Maggie and Bento walk up the path.  Bento still had his full head of hair that was only tinged with grey, while Maggie's hair had turned from rose gold to shining silver.  They walked slowly, Maggie holding Bento's hand and guiding him gently.  His eyesight was deteriorating.  Maggie was still spry and kept a busy schedule helping out with numerous charity functions. They paused at the waterfall and were laughing happily together, perhaps reminiscing about their meeting.  I had tried to make the waterfall to resemble the beautiful Victoria Falls.

They made their way towards the house as our neighbours came through the white gate.  Everyone settled in the comfortable living room, sinking into the oversized sofa and armchairs.  I set them up with drinks and snacks and turned on the television.

"Oh my gosh.  There he is!" Maggie exclaimed.

"Fi-Fi, Jussy come on down.  Oscars are starting!" I called out.

There was a clatter on the stairs and Sophia and Justine hurried down.  Justine still managed to get my heart thumping.  Her hair was shorter now, but still had that beautiful sheen and her eyes still sparkled with laughter--the lightest blue with those dark lashes. Bennie had inherited those.

All eyes were glued to the scene on the television.  There was Morris, standing tall and proud in his immaculate tuxedo, stepping away from the limousine.  He had a few laugh lines around his eyes, but otherwise, he looked, with his mischievous smile, as youthful as ever.  He waved to the crowd of spectators and walked onto the red carpet.

"Just arriving is the devilishly handsome Morris Jackson."  The T.V. announcer's beautiful face came on the screen.  "Nominated for Best Actor for his magnificent role in the drama, Beyond Time, Morris has certainly moved ahead in his career since his first film, The Zulu King.  That was not nominated for any awards, but it did launch his career."

"Yes," replied another male announcer. "Let's hope this talented and big-hearted man gets the recognition he deserves today. I heard that after that first film, he donated a substantial amount of money to a school in Zimbabwe and to the private game reserve where the filming occurred."

There was another shot of Morris talking to some fans and signing autographs.

"Oh, I just can't believe it," Maggie said in an excited voice.

After what seemed a long time, as I wasn't really interested in the parade of glamorous people in expensive dresses, the awards presentation began. We were all on the edge of our seats when finally we heard the nominations for Best Actor. The camera panned the audience and Maggie yelled out again, "Oh look, there are Chaz and Sugar!"

Chaz was as bald as ever, his face lined with wrinkles and Sugar, still with her long rasta braids, looked as if she was about to jump out of her seat.

"Oh I wish she would stand up so I can see what she is wearing," Maggie said. We all laughed. "It's probably something she made with her sewing machine out of an old curtain."

"And will be a fashion trend next week," Sophia added.

"Shhh, shhh," Bento said. "Listen up now."

The names were read out and then the elegant actress said, as she opened the envelope, "And the winner is…" there was a pause that seemed to go on forever and I noticed I was holding my breath, then I heard: "Morris Jackson."

We were all screaming and laughing, then we all stood up, hugging one another. The cameras panned the audience in Hollywood and we could see Sugar and Chaz. They looked as if they were screaming and laughing and hugging as well. Morris was beaming as he stood up and walked onto the stage. I can't remember what he said, but I'm sure it was witty and eloquent. I do remember him giving thanks to me, for what I wasn't sure. After all, what had I done but be with him on this roller coaster ride of life?

Then Morris paused. He looked out at the audience to where Chaz and Sugar sat. He coughed and briefly told of how he had been left abandoned in a cardboard box. He had been rescued and given the finest opportunity in life, thanks to his parents.

"I hope, in my own way, I can make such a profound difference by helping those less fortunate, and by being an environmental advocate.  Thank you for this honour."

He held up the beautiful Oscar and as he did so, the sleeve of his white silk shirt fell back and exposed a thick, beaded bracelet.  I was touched that he had kept that symbol of his birth mother with him through the years.  His gaze swept the audience again, and it seemed as if he could connect with every person there.

He delivered his message: "May we all embrace the spirit of my birthplace; the spirit of Ubantu - Humanity towards others.  My friend and brother Sammy and I were told that this blessing and wisdom came from our great-grandfathers.

"Never be afraid to do what is right.  Your voice is important.  Hamba lami.  Go with me, God."

*The End*

# Glossary

Amadlozi - ancestors/spirits
Badza - hoe
Bayethe - Zulu salute to the king
Beer-boep - beer belly
Baobab  - deciduous tree of central Africa
Boerewors - sausage
Bwana - boss
Chief Gambo - Chief of the Matabele, died 1916
China - my friend
Chiboolies - beer
Chibuku – African beer
Chongololo - a millipede
Chuffed - pleased
Doek - headscarf
Donga - ditch
Down South - South Africa
F.N. - Belgian submachine gun
Hamba kahle - go, stay well
Hambe lami - go with me
Hukus - chickens
Ibizo lakho - what is your name?
Ijuba - dove
Ikona - no
Impisi - hyena
Induna - chief
Iziko induba - don't worry
Ja - yes
Kia - African hut
Kanjani - how are you?
Kopje - hill
Kraal - African village
Lekker - nice
Mãe - Portuguese for mother
Maiwee - cry of distress
Matabele - African tribe in Southern region of Zimbabwe
Manje - now
Mealie - corn or maize

Mfundisi - priest or missionary
Mopani flies - gnat-like stingless bee species
Msasa - a tree of central Africa

Mushi - wonderful
Muti - medicine
Pai - Portuguese for father
Picinini - African child
Sadza - cooked cornmeal – a staple food in Zimbabwe
Shumba - lion
Shuppa - don't bother
Skelm - troublemaker
Shamwari - my friend
Siyabonga - we thank you
Sindebele - language of the Matabele
Stoep - a porch/veranda
Tekkies - an athletic shoe, a sneaker
Terrs - terrorists
Ubuntu - humanity towards others
Veldskoens - leather shoe
Voetsak - go away

## ABOUT THE AUTHOR

Christine Gordon was born in what is now Zimbabwe and, after teaching primary school, left the country in 1979.  After living in Canada, she travelled to Mexico, Costa Rica, the Bahamas, and Florida.  She resides in Santa Barbara County, in the small beach town of Carpinteria.  She has worked on charter boats, trained llamas and has taught yoga for thirty years.  This is her third novel.

See https://www.facebook.com/themourningdoveseries/

## ABOUT THE ARTIST

Fran was born and grew up on the family farm in Kenya. In 1963, they moved to South Africa.  In 1973, she attended The Teacher's College in Bulawayo, Rhodesia, where she befriended Christine. In 2003, after teaching for twenty-two years, she and her family moved to the United Kingdom. She began studying Fine Art at the University for the Creative Arts in 2008, and graduated in 2012, with a BA in Fine Art. She works as an artist, teacher, and illustrator. (See www.gazoonka.com)

www.ingramcontent.com/pod-product-compliance
Lightning Source LLC
Chambersburg PA
CBHW050945050726
47592CB00007B/2441